EMPTY SOUL FOR HIRE

To McKnight

Thanks for the support.

Jaime Waggoner
2013

EMPTY SOUL FOR HIRE

James H. Waggoner

AuthorHouse™
1663 Liberty Drive
Bloomington, IN 47403
www.authorhouse.com
Phone: 1-800-839-8640

© 2013 by James H. Waggoner. All rights reserved.

No part of this book may be reproduced, stored in a retrieval system, or transmitted by any means without the written permission of the author.

Published by AuthorHouse   02/19/2013

ISBN: 978-1-4817-1682-6 (sc)
ISBN: 978-1-4817-1683-3 (e)

Library of Congress Control Number: 2013902662

This book is printed on acid-free paper.

Because of the dynamic nature of the Internet, any web addresses or links contained in this book may have changed since publication and may no longer be valid. The views expressed in this work are solely those of the author and do not necessarily reflect the views of the publisher, and the publisher hereby disclaims any responsibility for them.

This is a work of fiction. Names, characters, businesses, places, events and incidents are either the products of the author's imagination or used in a fictitious manner. Any resemblance to actual persons, living or dead, or actual events is purely coincidental.

For
Blanche M. and James R.
Thank you for the childhood of a lifetime.

To My Children,
If you can dream it, then you can achieve it.
Follow all of your dreams and don't accept mediocrity.
It's crowded at the bottom but lonely at the top!

One

My watch read 11:17 PM PST. As the second hand continued to move, time was running out for the pathetic body before me. Carter Wilson had crossed the path of someone he thought would go gentle into the night. How wrong he was. Most people had no idea of my true identity. To most people I was Lance Goodman, the manager with the friendly smile, at the local Kinkos, always helpful and with a story or two to tell. To a small group of men and women, I had another identity. I did favors for rich people who considered themselves untouchable. But if you crossed them, they would certainly reach out and touch you. As I bound Carter's legs and arms to a chair in an abandoned warehouse in the run-down industrial area of Carson, California, he begged for his life. He saw rodents running about, smelt the scents of rotted metal and damp concrete. His cries for help went unheard. It was just him and me. He stopped screaming and tried pleading:

"Please don't kill me. I know who you are. We can work this out."

"No I don't think we can."

"I'll pay you double whatever they're paying you."

"Is that right? And who is they that you think is paying me?"

"I know those pompous bastards! That bunch in Pasadena isn't happy how I handled their money." He paused; a glimmer of hope showed in his eyes. "I can get them back their filthy money."

"You haven't gotten it back for them so far; why should they believe you now?"

I punched him in his mouth and his lips started to bleed. He spit and looked at me angrily. "Is that all you got?"

I came in close enough to smell his unruly breath:

"You haven't even begun to feel the pain that's coming."

His bleeding lips spat out vulgar words as I continued setting up the meeting between him and his savior of choice. He could see the tools of my trade being arranged on a metal table. I turned to face the short potbellied begging man as he watched me reach for a pair of metal snips and a blowtorch. I sat down in front of him and said politely, "You shouldn't have been so greedy." Then I cut off his first finger. Blood spurt out until I applied the blowtorch to the wound. Loud screams echoed through the abandoned warehouse, with no one to hear them but the rats. With no one to answer but the SoCal winds of night.

"Listen we can fix this." He was begging again. "We can go to the bank first thing in the morning."

"Sorry, I've got a yoga class in the morning."

His ring finger fell to the floor and I punched him again. I was sick of his begging and useless pleading. My iPhone buzzed. It was a text message: SMS—IS THE JOB DONE? I replied—IN PROGRESS. SMS—KEEP UP THE GOOD WORK.

Wires from a Concorde battery led to clamps attached to Carters wrists and ankles. I flipped the switch of the power source and Carter

Empty Soul for Hire

felt 45,000 volts of electricity tear through his body. Watching his body shake and his head flop from side to side gave me shivers of pure joy. I flipped the switch off, and then on again, then off, then walked over to him. "Do you want to know if that's all I got?" I asked.

I took a drink of Gatorade as I listened to Carter gasp for his breath. I took a construction hammer and pounded both his shoulders. The sound of his bones cracking was music to my ears. I crushed both of his wrists and then all his toes. Carter was barely breathing at this point; he looked up at me dripping sweat and blood and somehow mustered the strength to say "Go ahead muthafucka just kill me."

"Nice of you to surrender" I told him. "But I get to decide when it's over." Tears puddled in his stupid eyes, He spit some blood.

"Go to hell!" he said weakly.

That was it. I had heard the slob's last vulgar word of the evening. If I was lucky I still had time to catch "Jimmy Kimmel Live." I scanned the table for my lullaby medicine and filled and tapped the syringe. I squeezed the syringe to check for air bubbles. A tiny bit squirted from the tip. I turned around and Carter, both eyes swollen almost shut, was looking around the warehouse for any sign of the cavalry coming to his rescue. No one was coming, nothing but his nightcap. I slightly bent his right arm and looked into his eyes just before I injected the cocktail of barbiturate, paralytic, and potassium. I said, "You could have avoided all this by giving my clients back their investments. Sweet dreams, you greedy bastard."

His body wiggled as the lethal drug entered his wrecked body and flowed in his greedy bloodstream. Amused by the thought that the local rats would die from the meat I had left them, I cleaned up the job site and got on the 110 freeway. As I got close to Los Feliz Hills, I pulled out my iPhone 5 and sent a text message—JOB COMPLETE SMS. The reply came seconds later—TRANSFER COMPLETE. As I pulled into my garage, a breath of relief and anger exhaled from my body. I enjoyed what I did but I was getting tired of dealing with the worthless people of this world who had no honor, no respect, who kept taking with no expectations of retaliation. I sunk into my couch just as Jimmy Kimmel introduced his first guest—Matthew McConaughey.

Two

"**What am I going** to do this beautiful California day?" Jordan asked her empty Westwood condo.

I need a manicure and a pedicure, but I don't feel like wasting my one day off listening to a bunch of tiếng Việt. The only English they knew was "You want pedicure and manicure? What color you like?"

I'll call my girl Miriam and see what trouble we can get into; I knew she was always down to shop, eat, and gossip. The voice of Beyoncé's "Love on Top" rang in my ear. Miriam answered super excited: "What's up girl, where you been?"

"I've been here, silly; you the one so busy with the recruiting business."

"True, true. I got to make a living in La La Land and I prefer the legal way."

We both laughed.

"Girl, what are you doing today?" I asked

"I have to meet a client at 2, but that's it."

"Can you reschedule? I feel like hanging out."

"Jordan, now you messing with my money. Let me see what I can do."

It was just like Miriam to make things seem more than what they were. Seriously, if this client was all that why wasn't she meeting her at the first hour of business like 9 or 10 AM? I got up and started cleaning up my condo and doing laundry. I turned on the television, where the most anticipated election of my lifetime was on every channel. I was tired of it already. Neither candidate was going to live up to his word as president. Politicians spoke to get voters' attention along the campaign trail, but along their own trails they had so many favors to repay that the voters would come in fourth place at best. Half of America wouldn't admit it, but they didn't want a black president in office for another four years, plain and simple. They worry he's going to run up the deficit and drive unemployment through the roof. Never mind history and how we got in this mess. How soon we forget the housing bubble burst and the unemployment rate under the previous administration. The Republican candidate was a robotic idiot who couldn't remember what he said from one minute to the next. So how was he going to run the United States? Better yet, who was going to run him? If he got elected, without a doubt America would be in another war and more jobs would be shipped overseas. I'll probably vote for the write-in candidate, LOL. My cell phone buzzed, and a picture of Miriam appeared on the screen.

"Jordan Hughes. How may I help you?" I answered.

"Oh please, you know it's me. Why are you playing?"

I laughed. Miriam said, "I'm yours for the rest of the day, what we doing?"

"I was thinking we could meet at the Grove for lunch and wing it from there."

"The Grove sounds good girl; see you at noon, and wear your best jeans."

"All of my jeans are the best; you know that."

"Yea yea, see you at noon."

When we disconnected I went to my closet and looked over the potentials; True Religion, 7 for all mankind, Cookie Johnson, Lucky's, Dereon's, and my all-time favorite Roberto Cavalli because he fit my wagon so nicely. I needed a special top because I knew Miriam was going to be dressed to the hilt, and I'm running the show today. I pulled out an unworn Versace shirt and put on a pair of Christian Louboutin, perfect. I turned the television off and clicked on my old-school Sony reel-to-reel and let Marvin Gaye take over my condo. I jumped in the shower and let the steam calm me. I could see downtown L.A. from my bathroom window. I thought about the last time I had been in a relationship and, damn, it had been a minute. Dating in the city of Angels brought on so much frustration I had given up on it and retreated to happy hours, a few matchmaking attempts by friends and family, and occasional friends with sex benefits. But here I was, ready to give it a try again. I loved Miriam, but not enough to trade in the joy of a sweet love stick for a pair of lips. The Grove usually has some fine men walking around. Nowadays, you don't know which side of the tracks brothers are on, but let's see what today brings.

Three

"**Welcome to Kinkos**" **was** my standard greeting to customers. All walks of life came through that door at all times of the day. There were your college students working on that last-minute project, projecting attitude because the printers weren't fast enough. The up-and-coming business men or women printing business cards with embellished information, even though they had no plans, no capital, no techniques, just a hazy idea of owning a business and achieving the La La Land dream of untold riches. The saddest was the freelance artist who was clueless about art and had no talent but was eager to throw some bullshit together then try to sell it. At best they had taken 18 credit hours of art yet felt they were destined to be the next Pablo Picasso. All in all, this part of my life was stress-free and risk-free. I had been helping a customer for a couple of weeks with a billboard he was working on. Mr. Crepts was a mild fellow with grand ideas of making it big in Hollyweird. I listen to his ambition and the stories of who he had supposedly met and who he was allegedly connected to, all the while thinking to myself that if he only knew what my life was really about he would run screaming from the store. I told him stories of my career in the Army and the dangerous missions I went on. He was intrigued by my stories and said I was brave. He said he couldn't imagine killing another human being. Then I would just laugh and say "You get used to it."

"Good morning Mr. Crepts, how are you today?"

"Another day above ground Lance, how are you?"

"Life's good, beautiful weather here compared to our neighbors on the East Coast."

"Yea, they're getting beat up pretty bad now from that hurricane."

"Mr. Crepts, what are we going to work on today?"

"Lance, I think I've changed the direction slightly, take a look at this."

Mr. Crept had changed his design. His original piece was a crowd of people dancing in the streets under what looked like an orchestra featuring Frank Sinatra, Miles Davis, John Coltrane, Lucille Ball, and Redd Foxx. I asked him, "What happened to your original piece?"

"I didn't think it was enough. Why? Did you like it?"

"I loved it. I thought we could bring some color to it to highlight your theme. But hey, you're the artist; I'm here to help you."

"Thanks Lance, but this here is what's going to get me into Hollyweird as you call it."

His new design looked like the city of L.A. in a scene from the old cartoon Jetsons. The design had cartoon pictures of Steven Spielberg in a bullet-like limousine and Denzel in a pudgy jet with Al Pacino. But the one that stood out the most was the picture of Whitney Houston riding alongside Marilyn Monroe. I didn't know exactly where Mr. Crept was going with his design, but it's his dream and I'm here to help the dreams of the many come alive in my shop of PC design computers, printers, and drafting tables. After Mr. Crept, the rest of the day was moderately busy—going over the monthly receipts, checking work schedules and planning the upcoming monthly specials. Then I was rudely interrupted by Sydney Williams . . .

"Mr. Goodman, sorry I'm late. My audition ran a little over."

I looked up to see the bubbly aspiring star standing in the door of my office.

"Okay Sydney, but sooner or later you need to decide—Hollyweird or working wages?"

"Mr. Goodman, you know I'm going to be the next Julia Roberts, and I'm not sleeping my way to the top like you might think."

"I don't think anything. I just know, as I'm sure you do, a lot of people come to this great state with hopes and dreams of being big stars. They work meaningless jobs without seriously considering their futures, thinking one day they're going to be the next Angelina Jolie or Eddie Murphy. Today's generation was raised to expect instant gratification and success, not like the old days of hard work and dedication. Hollyweird chews up the best of them and when it's done with you, it will spit you out without nothing left on your bones. By then you're mentally drained, embarrassed, or worse—strung out with an addiction so bad you can't get a college degree or learn a tech trade to make a decent living."

"Mr. Goodman, that won't be me, trust me."

As she clocked in to start her shift, I shook my head and silently wished her all the best. The sun was beginning to leave tracks across the sky and bid itself good night in the Pacific Ocean. The city was ready to come alive for the night and I felt like being a part of it for a change. I hadn't been out in so long I didn't know where the hot spots were anymore. Guess I'll just end up where I end up and see what happens.

Four

The Grove was lively just as I expected. Everyone was shopping, people-watching, eating on the terraces of their favorite restaurants or standing in line to watch the latest movie. I sat outside on the terrace of Morel's French Steakhouse waiting for Miriam to arrive. I ordered a Rum Manhattan to sip on while I took in the brothers. After Janet Jackson dated one of the elite from Qatar, international brothers had come on the scene almost overnight. They were mostly handsome, tanned, and well groomed; mostly tall with the extra allure of deep "oil" pockets. There was nothing like an attractive brother, local or from far away. I went for the 6 ft 2 in to 6 ft 4in light chocolate ones that looked like the British guy from "Takers," Idris Elba. That brother was fine, he had become the Billy Dee of his era, passing Henry Simmons and Shemar Moore. Come to find out Henry Simmons was said to be riding both sides of the track, so I'll take him off the list. What a waste. When Idris speaks, I'm sure a lot of women's juices start to flow and when he flashes those pearly whites it make you want to kiss him so softly. My, my, my either I need to get me some or this Rum Manhattan is a little strong. I saw Miriam walking up to the restaurant. She was dressed to impress, with 7 jeans on, Jimmy Choo pumps, and a top I'd seen in Saks by Chanel. She had her Louis Vuitton clutch around her wrist and her aviator frames on.

"Hey girl, sorry I'm late."

She wasn't sorry; we'd been friends far too long. She always showed up late so she could be in the spotlight.

"Oh girl it's no problem. I was sitting here just enjoying the sights."

"Yes indeed, it was a brother in the Kiehl store trying to holla but his jeans were too tight and he looked like he had on make-up."

"Girl if he wearing make-up who knows what else he wears."

We both laughed. Hanging out with Miriam was always relaxing. We had met in college while attending the University of Spoiled Children aka USC. I majored in business finance and she majored in human resources; we took a couple of classes together and built our relationship from there.

"So what's up girl? I can't believe the bank let you off."

"Girl I just needed some me time. It's been busy in there with the low mortgage rates. Everybody's trying to either buy a new home or refinance."

"In this economy, I'm just thankful both of us are respectfully employed and not on the pole."

"I know that's right, having smelly dudes feel on you for ten dollars."

I knew exactly what Miriam was talking about. Out here, thanks to the Terminator, jobs were few and far between. The housing scandals and Ponzi get-rich schemes have cost so many their well-earned fortunes. Today is about me, but I'm not crazy; I need to keep saving my pennies for a rainy day. I'm an attractive, educated, young and single black female that has her act together. These L.A. men need to quit living in fantasy land and get their shit together. Unplug the video games, stop thinking braids and throwback jerseys are sexy. Get a real job and quit watching those blockbuster movies thinking they're going to be the next Nino Brown or Tony Montana. Oh my God, if I meet another man over 30 trying to be a rapper, I'm going to scream. Damn, it would be nice to meet a decent brother with his shit together. I'd even consider one with a baby mama or an ex-wife, but just be decent and straight.

"So, Jordan what are we doing today?"

"I was thinking we could eat, shop, and hit a party or two tonight. I heard Jamie Foxx was having a private party at the Conga Room. You know we need to make a grand entrance to let these scandalous chicks know who the boss is."

"Girl, I know that's right, and hopefully it will be some cuties in the house."

"Okay, so what's our first stop?"

"Let's hit Banana Republic. They have a nice grey pencil skirt in there I want to try on. See if I can squeeze my tight ass in a 6? LOL."

"Jordan, you need to stop pretending you don't have hips girl. You know that ass needs an 8 and my plump rump pushing a 12 or 14."

"Miriam, what happen to you going to kickboxing?"

"Nothing, I stop going. Besides, work has been picking up. I have two new clients with recruitment needs and they have quick turnaround times, so I just haven't had the time. Hell I barely have time to get some loving. Between my schedule and Scott's it's been rough on a sister."

"How is Scott doing? I haven't heard you talk much about him since he started working for Sony pictures."

Empty Soul for Hire

"He's okay, not too happy with the job at the moment. He feels more like a gofer than an executive. He's always at a function and gets home late."

"Well that's what he wanted, right? I'm sure things will settle down soon for him. Tell him I said hi."

"I will do that."

"Welcome to Banana Republic, our special today is 30 percent off your entire purchase and an extra 15 percent if you open a BR credit card today. My name is Khan if you need anything."

"Girl, did you hear how sexy he sounded, and I don't think he's gay."

"Yes I did, I was already in my purse pulling out a business card to give to him, LOL."

"You are a mess Jordan, so fresh."

"Whatever! It's been a real minute since I've had some maintenance and my check engine light is on."

"Let him help you with that grey skirt you mention and feel him out."

"Hmmm, we'll see. You know I don't go after men. Men come after me, and they better come correct."

"Ma'am what size are you looking for?"

"Can I try a 6 and an 8?"

"Of course, but I think a 6 would fit just right. Here we go, a 6 and 8 for the pretty young lady."

In the dressing room, I began to pull my jeans down to try the skirt on when I heard Khan's deep voice ask, "How's that 6 working for you?"

I responded politely: "Fitting just right, as you said."

"Well come out girl, let me see."

Let him see, is he joking? He's coming on a little too strong, but what the hell. I stepped out in the main area of the dressing room. He was standing there with black slacks on, a blue shirt and a pin dot tie, sporting what look to be a pair of Ferragamo boots.

"That skirt looks really good, did you have a top in mind to go with it?"

"Actually I didn't; what do you recommend?"

"One minute, I'll be back."

When he returned, he had a light pink blouse to match perfectly with the skirt, and he had the right size.

"Here is a medium; I thought a small would be too tight."

Damn if he isn't gay; he definitely has an eye for fashion.

"The medium is fine. Thank you," I answered.

"Let me know if you need anything else," he said smiling.

Miriam came running in the dressing room

"Jordan, what the hell is going on in here? I saw Mr. BR come back here."

"Nothing. He was checking on me. Did you think I was back here having sex?"

"Don't act brand new, like you haven't had sex in public."

"True, true," I laughed.

I did like the skirt and the top Mr. Khan chose, so I bought both. But I didn't apply for the credit card. As he checked me out, I could see his eyes making contact in between scanning the two items. So I went for it: "Are you married, Khan?" I flirtatiously asked.

He smiled; dental work was in check. That was a plus in L.A. He replied, "No I'm not married; are you married?"

"No I'm not. Here's my business card. Call me sometime; let's get a drink or a bite to eat."

"Sounds good Ms. Hughes"

When we got outside Miriam couldn't wait to clown me.

"What happen to I don't go after men . . . men come after me?"

"Girl, you're too funny. I just gave him my card. Dang."

"Yea okay, sounds like that check-engine light will be off soon."

I laughed, knowing that if Mr. BR played it right he definitely would be the next service mechanic to give me a tune-up, balance and rotate my tires. LOL.

Five

L.A. traffic is like a woman, can't live with it and can't live without it. I had just left Kinkos headed home to freshen up before I hit the scene. The 5 Freeway was jam-packed, so I tuned in to KJLH and let the classic R&B take me home. The radio station was playing tunes from the '80s: Anita Baker was soothing how it had been so long and that she wouldn't be neglected or denied, the pleasure of your kisses, the pleasure of your smile, I think you take me for granted, that I'll always be here. Just because I love you it doesn't mean I won't disappear, been so long. That was music. Today the artists were about bump and grind sex or disrespecting one another shooting and killing. There was no love in the music today. Even jazz was falling off: the smooth jazz station was becoming an R&B station. Nothing like the old sounds of Miles, Coltrane, Charlie Parker, Kenny G, or the sexy Asian pianist Keiko Matsui are on the airwaves anymore. I had seen her play some years ago at the Newport Beach Jazz Festival and she brought the house down. I was coming up to my exit and I got this feeling I had been having lately; a feeling of loneliness and wondering if I'd ever be in a committed relationship again. It had become difficult to mask my identity behind Kinkos, disappearing all hours of the night and for days at a time. The last relationship I was in I got too comfortable and nearly blew my cover behind LL-oooh-vee-eee. Londen Coles, I thought was going to be my wife. We had all the essentials to a successful relationship. She was educated, didn't have a lot of baggage, and she was fun. We would sit and talk on the phone for hours about random stuff, real life, politics, gay and straight relationships, even sports. She knew I was a die-hard OKC Thunder fan and she loved her Los Angeles Lakers. I remember the day she came into Kinkos like it was yesterday. She walked in wearing a navy blue suit with a pair of shoes that had red bottoms and I remember asking a stupid question after my standard store greeting:

"Why are the bottoms of your shoes red?" I asked.

She laughed so hard it got everyone's attention in the store.

"Sir, you need to get out more" is all she could say.

I didn't get it at the time. It wasn't until I saw a fashion show on TV one night that I learned about the infamous Christian Louboutin. Londen had walked around the store for a while before coming to the front counter. When she approached the counter, her beauty was mesmerizing. Her light brown skin tone was impeccable, not a blemish, scar, or pimple in sight. Her eyelashes were long and her hair was curly and long. She was about 5 ft 4 in in height, and from what I could see toned and in shape, probably a size 6.

I got the idea she was sizing me up too. Then she asked. "I need to print out a placard for a job fair; do you have someone that can help me?"

"How big do you want it to be? Is it going on a wall or an easel?" I asked.

"It's going on an easel."

"Oh okay, you probably want to print that on our 25 white foam sheet. It's light but durable, and inexpensive."

"How long would it take to complete it? I think a 4' x 8' would be big enough."

"Do you have an electronic copy of the design?"

"I have it on a memory stick."

As she handed me the memory stick, I made it a point to lightly touch her hand, which was silky smooth and soft, not one day of hard work on those hands. "Thank you, let's take a look. What's the title?"

"It's the only file on there."

"There we go; let's see what we have. You work at the chamber of commerce?"

"Yes sir."

Career woman . . . . check, attractive . . . . check. The placard was designed professionally. She was the marketing director at the chamber of commerce and the job fair was for new college graduates in accounting and information technology.

"We can finish this for you in 3 to 5 days. Is that soon enough?"

"That will work, Mr. Goodman."

"Please call me Lance."

"Thank you. Lance."

After I entered her order in the system, I asked for her telephone number as a point of contact. She gave me her business card. As she turned to walk away, I politely asked, "Mind if I call you for lunch one day?"

"Let's get the placard finished and we'll see about that, Lance."

She didn't break stride as she spoke and like that was gone. I'd have one of my employees complete her project in one day, but I wouldn't call until after 3 days. When I called the number on her card, another voice answered.

"Ms. Coles' office how may I help you?"

"May I speak to Londen Coles?"

"May I ask who's calling?"

"Lance Goodman."

"One moment please."

"Good afternoon Lance; is my placard complete?"

"Yes it is; you can stop by the store anytime, or I can bring it to you if you like."

"That won't be necessary; I'll have my assistant stop by and pick it up."

Let the chess match begin. She didn't want to address the question of lunch again so to avoid it, she was sending her assistant to pick up the placard. Okay, I'll move my pawn first. I'd play this game a few times and soon I'll have her heart and her king in my hand.

"That will be fine. Your placard is ready for pickup."

"Thank you, Mr. Goodman. Have a good day."

"Likewise."

We disconnected.

Six

It had been a week since Londen Coles' assistant picked up the placard. She hadn't called me and I didn't want to seem desperate. In the dating game you had to move strategically but effectively. So I called her and asked about the placard and how the job fair had gone.

"Ms. Coles office how may I help you?"

"This is Lance Goodman at Kinkos is Ms. Coles available?"

"One moment please."

"Hi Mr. Goodman, how are you?"

"I'm well; I wanted to follow up with you and see how the job fair went and if the placard was to your satisfaction?"

"Mr. Goodman is that really what you called for?"

I couldn't believe she had just switched on me.

"Now that you mention it; no it isn't. I called to ask you to lunch or dinner."

"Mr. Goodman, I really prefer to keep my personal life separate from my professional relationships."

"The project is complete, right?"

"This particular project is. But you don't think I'll come to Kinkos again?"

"I don't know; will you? How often do you have job fairs and need placards?"

"Not very often, but the potential is there. I'll tell you what Mr. Goodman I have an opening on my calendar this coming Thursday. Does that work for you?"

"That works, what time and where?"

"You asked me out, so you tell me. I have two and a half hours."

"Let's meet at the Boa Steakhouse on Sunset at 5 PM."

"It's a date. See you then Mr. Goodman."

"Please, call me "Lance."

I woke up and went to the gym to work out before meeting Londen. When I got back I showered and shaved. I put on my Lucky jeans and a Hugo Boss button-down shirt. I like to be early to meetings, especially first dates so I arrived at the Boa Steakhouse fifteen minutes early. When I walked in, the maître d' greeted me and said, "Sir, your party is waiting for you."

Damn, she's here already. I like this woman already. When I got to the table, she looked up and said, "I like a man that's early."

"I like a woman that's on time."

Empty Soul for Hire

"Excuse me, I'm early Lance."

I laughed and sat down. The waiter took our drink order. I ordered a Coke Zero no ice and she ordered a Perrier.

During a brief silence, Londen reviewed the situation. What does this man want? He's definitely fine as hell; a mix between Blair Underwood and the brother that wrote the Personal Conversations book—Hill Harper. His body looks tight; I can tell he works out. Nice fade haircut and the light eyes are making my cakes a little moist. But I'm sure there's a story to his story, same as all the other brothers in L.A., pretending to be something or someone they're not trying to impress.

"Londen!"

The sound of her name pulled her out of her daydream. Her quick smile was a reflex.

"I was asking how you are?"

"I'm well Lance. And you?"

"Great actually."

"Yeah? And why is that?"

"I'm on a date with you, something I didn't think would happen."

"I didn't think it would either to be honest. You're not exactly my type."

"What is your type? A suit and tie executive? A ball player? A doctor? Don't let the Kinkos job fool you, my lady."

"Aren't we smelling ourselves today? And just so you know, I don't date athletes. But the other two mentioned are definite possibilities."

"Excuse me then."

"You're excused."

The waiter brought our drinks and took our order. Londen ordered the Maryland crab cake and I ordered halibut with string beans. While we waited, Londen became very straightforward. She asked, "What is it that you're looking for, Lance?"

She was definitely a chess player. I wasn't expecting that direct a question; I replied as best I could: "I'm not looking for anything in particular. I have a happy life at the moment, but if someone comes along who could increase my happiness, I'd gladly welcome her. Let me ask you, what are you looking for?"

"Everything you just said sounds good, but let's face it, dating is painfully hard in L.A. Where I work I need to be able to have someone that can speak on any topic that comes up. And by topic I don't mean when the next Madden game comes out or what mixed tape is dropping. Some, not all brothers feel they have to have every race but black in tow once they make it. Not knocking it, just speaking on what I see. I don't know much about you other than you work at Kinkos."

"Actually, I own the store," I said, modestly I hope."

"Well," she said, toying with her glass of Perrier. "I am impressed."

She was partly right. A lot of brothers were chasing Caucasian, Latina, or Asian women, laying around making excuses for not working better jobs, and still holding Madden tournaments on the weekends. L.A was a beast in the dating game. I had to play it, but I refused to buy into it. I knew there were single black females out there with their acts together, and I also knew these same women looked down on brothers in general. If the man wasn't suited to the nines and pushing a nice whip, very unlikely he'd get their attention. Stereotypes and bad impressions had plagued our culture for generations and sad to say we still fell short. Unlike my white friends, who looked at women in a totally different light. White men didn't usually fall for all the glitz and glam; they were simple, more direct. They met, talked, found similarities, and took chances. Not us, brothers came with the mile-long checklist, childhood baggage, adult baggage, previous relationship baggage but expected the person in front of us to be picture perfect with none of the things we were bringing to the table.

"I'll tell you what, Londen, after lunch I'll give you my number and you can decide if I'm worth your time and we can take it from there." Londen looked surprised at my suggestion.

Perhaps she couldn't believe I hadn't tried to convince her she should go out with me. Those days were long gone for me. I knew my worth. And Kinkos was certainly not the measure of that worth. I owned a business, was educated, single, had no kids, but I did have a small bit of baggage. Would Londen learn about that baggage depended on her? For now I'm the owner of a Kinkos.

I was pulled out of my daydream when my iPhone buzzed.

SMS—A NEW PACKAGE, ARE YOU AVAILABLE?

SMS—YES

SMS—SUBJECT IS IN L.A. FOR 2 NIGHTS AND WILL BE AT A CLUB CALLED THE CONGA ROOM TONIGHT. A PICTURE WILL BE SENT SHORTLY.

I downloaded the picture of my new package. He was high-profile attorney from Tampa, Florida. He represented drug cartel lords from Colombia and had not done a good enough job in a recent federal hearing for Colombia's lead drug lord. This didn't sit well with my associates. The request was to torture him until he gave up certain information and the whereabouts of the preliminary witnesses he had paid to disappear so he could extort more money from the cartel as retainer fees. Well I guess I'm going to the Conga Room tonight.

I entered my place through the garage. The smell of el ranchero steak, black beans, and rice permeated the house. My housekeeper Catalina had cooked dinner for me before she left. Catalina comes three times a week to cook and clean for me. I met her when I first moved to L.A. She's like my mom and will definitely curse me out in a minute if things aren't right at the house. I never met a Latina woman that would curse you out so fast. She has her own system and best believe you better not intrude on it. After I got out of the shower, I looked in my closet to see how much damage I wanted to cause tonight. Did I want to go casual or did I want to hit the scene hard with a Versace suit, Vacheron watch, and my handcrafted Forzieri boots from the finest Italian artisans? There was a chance of seeing this high-profile attorney possibly tonight, and he needed to know I belonged in his league and wasn't just an L.A. pretender begging for his attention. Little did he know he'd soon be begging for his life. I got dressed in my suit, boots, and expensive Swiss timepiece then threw on a splash of Killian white spice. I would roll in the latest and greatest luxury sedan on the market—the Porsche Panamera.

When I pulled up to the Conga Room valet parking and the VIP line was wrapped around the building. I knew once the bouncer got a good look at the Panamera I wouldn't be waiting in that line. I left the Porsche with the valet and proceeded up the paved walkway to the line. When I got there, the bouncer looked me up and down to see if I was someone famous. I stepped to him; in the palm of my right hand I had two neatly folded one hundred dollar bills. As we shook hands I released the dead presidents into his hand, he unhooked the red rope, and I walked past the working class type waiting in line. I noticed a fine young lady with a black dress standing in line. I hoped she got in, but I had more pressing business with a certain attorney. The speakers inside the Conga Room were blasting Usher's "Let's Go." The dance floor was packed and the VIP sections were full. One of those exclusive sections was occupied by Phillip Bach, Esquire. He was my height and biracial. He wore a Hickory Freeman suit, a crisp white shirt with French cuffs, Burberry tie, and had a dozen groupies with his entourage. Several bottles of Ace of Spades on his table and he slowly pulled on a primo Churchill cigar. I walked to the bar and ordered a glass of peach ciroc and stood back to take in the crowd. Mr. Bach appeared harmless, his entourage loyal and protective as they fended off other groupies trying to get his attention. Phillip had no idea that the marco clients he represented were on to his despicable scheme and that they had arranged sweet and final revenge. Revenge the eminent attorney would no doubt consider excessive. I couldn't take him out in the middle of downtown L.A., of course. His entourage was too close and, there were too many witnesses. Anyway, I didn't work that way.

Seven

"**If I knew it was** going to be this chilly I wouldn't have worn this dress." I told Miriam.

"I know, and this line is insane."

"I thought my dress was short enough to get us to the front of the line but these women bring a whole new meaning to the word *short.*"

"We look like we're dressed for church compared to them."

Miriam was right; we didn't stand a chance with these 25-year-old prima donnas. They had on mini-skirts with 6-inch stilettos and boobs pushed up and damn near out. I did catch the gentlemen with the Porsche that walked right past our cold ass and through the VIP ropes. His suit was fitting nice but hell he's probably renting that car for the weekend and working in the mall. This is L.A.—after all.

Just before our asses froze, we got inside the club.

"It's about time. My goodness."

"They have it real nice in here, Jordan, and the sound system is on point. The eye candy isn't bad either."

"Eye candy? I don't see Scott in here."

We both laughed.

"No he's not in here. But I haven't seen an ugly brother yet. I'm going to keep on looking. When I get home, I'll wake him up and ride his love pole until I cum. Then I'll go to sleep and dream about the eye candy we saw tonight."

"Miriam, you're too funny. Let's get a drink."

When we got to the bar, the bartender was grinning like he had hit the lotto. "What can I get you ladies?" he asked.

"Two apple martinis please."

"Coming right up."

Waiting for our drinks, I noticed the gentlemen in the Porsche. He was a few people away from me, bobbing his head to Neyo's latest single. He wasn't talking to anyone or looking at anyone in particular, just taking in the scenery. He turned and saw me looking at him, so I just smiled, paid for our drinks, and walked away with Miriam.

"I saw the fine brother from the Porsche at the bar." I told her. She wasn't interested.

"Mmm, this martini is *strong*. Damn!"

"For eleven dollars it needs to be."

"Eleven dollars? Each?"

"Yes, Miriam. Calm down girl I got this."

We sipped on our drinks. Two guys walked up and asked us to dance. Both of us declined. It wasn't that type of night. We just wanted to relax and listen to some music.

It was getting late and I needed to get some information on Phillip Bach. I walked by the VIP section slowly and back to the bar. I waited a few seconds then turned to the bartender and said: "I need to close out Mr. Bach's tab."

Without hesitation, the bartender gave me a copy of the original credit card imprint and just like that I had verified his identity. With that information, Bach's countdown to death began to tick. As I was leaving the Conga Room, I saw the sweet young lady in the black dress again. She was with another female. I was there on business and I didn't have time to introduce myself. My associates liked my style, technique and timeliness so my reputation with them trumped this tempting hook-up.

When I pulled into Los Feliz Hills I was excited to get to work on Phillip Bach. Esq. I walked in and disarmed the alarm system, turned on the news to see the latest world calamities, news on the upcoming elections, unemployment rates, and the latest on the East Coast hurricane. TV news always confirmed my belief that the land of the free was truly becoming a vast pool of deranged people with no visible regard for life or freedom, especially other peoples. I turned my attention back to Phillip Bach. It was time to tap into his personal life, time to move forward with my mission. The high-profile attorney was staying at the Ritz-Carlton downtown, occupying the two top-floor suites; one for him and one for his three man security team. He had definitely built up his wealth from representing the Colombians. Amazing how much information you could gain from a credit card imprint. Attorney Bach was married with two children and lived in the luxurious sought-after gated community Cheval in Tampa, Florida. Homes there started in the $1 million price range and there were two golf courses. His law office was located in downtown Tampa at 100 North Tampa, the old Regions Bank building. He had a healthy seven-figure account with Bank of America, an American Express Black Card, an offshore account in Curacao, vacation properties in St. Tropez, Bora Bora, and Dubai. His luxurious Mangusta 80 yacht was tucked away at the nearby Clearwater Harbor Marina Club with a full staff ready to launch with a phone call's notice. With this information, I was ready to bring his lavish life style to an unyielding halt.

I woke up at 5 a.m. the next morning, did the INSANITY workout, and headed to the Downtown Ritz-Carlton to find out why Attorney Bach was in town. As I waited in the lobby, I saw one of his security men get off the elevator and survey the lobby, coffee shop, restaurant and newsstand. Then, I saw him speak into his wireless mic, no doubt informing the rest of the team the area was secure. Within seconds, two black Mercedes sedans pulled up to the front door of the Ritz; Attorney Bach and his security team exited the elevator, walked through the lobby casually and out the front door, and entered the two sedans. I folded up my L.A. Times and made my way to the sports utility vehicle I had rented this morning. It didn't take long to spot the two black sedans trailing each other on Figueroa St. I traveled four cars behind the attorney and his team. If his team was any good, they would spot the tail if I got any closer, so I played it safe. The two vehicles entered onto the 110 freeway towards San Pedro. Traffic was light on the freeway so I had to really lag and keep my speed at least 15 mph slower than theirs and I couldn't change lanes frequently. As we travelled towards one of L.A.'s oldest city, I called and checked on my staff at Kinkos.

"Thank you for calling Kinkos; this is Sydney how may I help you?"

"Good morning Sydney."

"Hi Mr. Goodman, how are you?"

"I'm well, how are things going?"

"No problems Sir. It was busy late last night with the college crowd and the Internet users, but other than that a normal day at Kinkos."

"Okay, I won't be in for a few days but I'm available on my cell if you guys need anything."

"Thank you Mr. Goodman; is there anything else?"

"No, that's it. Have a good one."

The journey on the 110 Freeway was coming to an end as we approached the Gaffey St. exit. Exiting was going to be tricky because there wasn't any traffic in this part of town this early. So as the two sedans took the south exit, I continued onto the north exit. Once I got on Gaffey, I would be able to navigate my whereabouts and locate them in my rearview mirror. I saw the two black sedans make a left turn but I wasn't certain of the street. When I felt it was safe, I made a U-turn in the middle of Gaffey and headed south to catch up with the high-profile attorney. I drove just over thirty allowing me to scan the streets for the two sedans. I came to 3rd St., no luck; cautiously proceeding to each street, I looked down 6th St. and saw the tail lights of one of the black sedans. I drove past 6th St. and made the left on 7th and drove down far enough until I felt I was close enough. I parked the SUV on a side street close to 6th St. and started walking towards where I saw the tail lights. We were by an old marina with boat slips. There were four or five small boats docked and a few older men fishing. A group of men was standing by the dock. Attorney Bach was talking to two other men. I moved close enough to hear them, pretending to be fascinated by the fishermen.

"Gentlemen, Banderas is resting nicely in the Federal Prison System and I doubt he'll see another day of freedom."

"What's make you so sure, Phil?"

"I have everything under control. You just need to keep your end of the deal."

"Our end isn't what concerns us. What concerns us is likely retaliation from the Colombian Cartel, they're going to catch on."

"Listen, the Cartel guys trust me with all of their legal affairs and have no reason to suspect any wrongdoing. As long as I tell them I'm filing appeals, they're happy with glimmers of hope."

"Phil, I hope you know what you're doing, this could get real messy; and stay out of the spotlight. Last night, you had too much going on at the Conga Room."

"How did you know?"

"This is our town, we know everything that goes on."

"I'm heading back to Tampa this evening."

"That's fine, you still need to stay low on the radar; high stakes right now. This isn't Vegas where you can cash in your chips and leave the tables. These kinds of stakes will leave generations to come fatherless and motherless, so stay low. We'll be in contact."

I saw the men part ways and return to their transportation. I walked back to my SUV, in no rush to get back on the freeway behind the black sedans. I had all the information needed. Now I needed to make my own flight arrangements to Tampa.

Eight

After the day I had yesterday, I was not feeling like work this morning; especially on a Saturday morning. Everybody in the bank would be either making deposit to cover checks so they didn't generate *insufficient funds* or asking dumb questions about simple banking. I just wasn't feeling it. When I got off the Blue Line, I was greeted by my daily homeless man:

"Hey pretty bank lady, how are you?"

"I'm fine Mr. Henry, here's ten dollars. Please go get something to eat and stop by the YMCA to shower."

"Thank you, pretty bank lady."

I wondered if Henry was his real name? It probably was since he's been telling me the same name for 3 years. When I walked into First Federal, I spoke to the bank managers and the security guards and a few coworkers I saw at the coffee pot. I had a few minutes before the doors open, so I went to the ladies room to finish getting myself together. Unlike the other women I worked with, I had a long clothing rotation. Judging from what I see most weeks, they all had a single pair of pants in black, gray, blue, and tan with an assortment of ugly blouses with one black blazer to go with everything. I knew most customers thought I was one of the managers. LOL. The doors opened promptly at 10 AM and the flow of customers wasn't too bad. I had just finished helping Ms. Britton, a regular customer that always managed to get me as a teller; she was funny to me. I didn't know what she did, but every week she cashed a check in the range of $160 to $180 dollars. After I would count her money out to her, she would recount it back to me. While she stood there counting her funds, I looked at the other customers waiting in line and for a second thought I saw the gentlemen with the Porsche Panamera from last night standing in the line. Ms. Britton thanked me and wished me a good day. There were 4 customers ahead of the fine gentleman from the Conga Room. I wasn't sure he'd get my window. Three tellers were working and the line was moving pretty quickly. Two customers left before Mr. Panamera would be at the front of the line. In a New York minute I told Barbara to take a break, sending Mr. Panamera to my window.

"Welcome to First Federal, how may I help you?"

"Good morning, I would like to make a withdrawal."

"How much are we withdrawing today and do you have your driver license?"

"Yes Ma'am. Sixty thousand, large bills please."

"One moment Sir, I will have to get a bank manager to sign off on this amount, it's over my limit."

"Good morning Mr. Goodman."

"Hi Tom, how's it going?"

"Very well. Thank you for banking with First Federal; have a good day."

"You as well."

"Okay Mr. Goodman, here are six wrapped stacks of $10,000 each. Would you like one of our private rooms to count your funds?"

"No thank you Ms. Hughes that won't be necessary."

If Mr. Panamera is on a first name basis with one of the bank managers, surely he wasn't renting the Porsche for the weekend and his account with us wasn't anything to blink at. I had to cast my line:

"Excuse me, if you don't mind me saying. I saw you last night at the Conga Room."

"Did you? Are you sure it was me?"

"I'm pretty sure it was. Didn't you pull up to the valet in a black Porsche Panamera?"

"Impressive! Yes I did, hi I'm Lance."

"Jordan Hughes"

"Nice to meet you Jordan, I'm kind of in a rush but here's my card; call me sometime."

"Thank you, I will do that. Have a nice day Mr. Goodman."

"Please call me Lance."

Lance walked away, and before my next customer got to my window I glanced at the business card. Lance Goodman, Kinkos store owner, Los Feliz Hills, Ca.

Nine

As I drove up the on ramp of the 110 Freeway to the Hawthorne Municipal Airport, I thought about Londen Coles and wondered how she was doing. I hadn't heard from her and my daily schedule had changed a lot since she'd come into Kinkos and we'd had lunch. My thoughts were interrupted by my cell buzzing.

SMS—STATUS

SMS reply—STILL GATHERING INTEL, ENROUTE TO SUBJECTS MAIN LOCALE

SMS—GREAT. KEEP US POSTED

SMS reply—ROGER THAT

When I arrived in the city of Hawthorne, I stopped by one of the oldest sandwich shops in L.A. County. It was family owned and they had the best turkey club sandwich this side of the Mississippi. I walked in; the lady behind the counter knew me well.

"Good afternoon Lance, the usual?"

"Yes Ma'am."

Empty Soul for Hire

I looked up at the television mounted on the wall; CNN was reporting on the trial of Colombian drug lord Banderas. The reporter stated that the trial was at a standstill as Banderas' attorney Phillip Bach continues to file appeals with no success. Meanwhile Banderas remained in federal custody with no pending bond as he's a serious flight risk. I grabbed my sandwich and thanked Ms. Holmes. When I arrived at the airport, the security guard recognized the Porsche Cayenne and waved me through. I parked in space 31, grabbed my duffle bag, and made it to the small quaint terminal. Sitting there, I pulled out my cell and made contact with my Tampa connect.

SMS—LANDING AT 5 PM LOCAL

SMS reply—YOUR ORDER IS READY

SMS—THANKS

While I was checking my messages and responding to emails from my suppliers for Kinkos, a small-framed female terminal associate walked up to me.

"Sir, the flight crew is ready."

"Thank you."

She grabbed my duffle bag and asked if I had any other luggage. I said "that's it." I walked out of the terminal and the golf cart driver greeted me—

"Welcome back Mr. Goodman."

"Thanks Clyde, how have you been?"

"Just working and keeping the lights on."

The catastrophic state of this economy was unforgiving and steadily sucking the life out of people leaving them with no hope.

Empty Soul for Hire

"I hear you man, thanks for the ride."

I paid my normal two hundred cart fare, though it was clearly included in the chartered service. It was really a tip for Clyde. As I boarded the 8-seat Gulfstream Jet, I was greeted by two flight attendants. From their skin tone, dark hair, and brassy voice tone I could tell they were of Middle-East decent.

"Welcome aboad Sir."

One was real slim and the other had her by fifteen pounds, both very pretty though. I took my seat in the rear of the jet.

"Cocktail Sir?"

"Yes please, peach Ciroc with two ice cubes."

"Yes sir, right away."

When the flight attendant returned I handed her a white sealed envelope. Inside was thirty-five thousand dollars cash for my round-trip chartered flight. My client account with Stratos Jet Charter was on a cash basis. The manifest was legit with the Federal Aviation Administration and the passenger list on board had no trace of Lance Goodman. I watched as the flight attendant took the sealed envelope. Her hands squeezed the corners of the envelope and then she said:

"Sir my name is Sabirah and my colleague is Rana. If you need anything during your flight, let one of us know. The meal for your flight is as you pre-ordered: grilled salmon with crab meat, asparagus, and carrots and a lemon bar tart. As you know, we have a full bar at your service."

"Thank you Sabirah."

When she turned around and walked away, I saw the fit of her skirt and the sexiness of her stride. I shook my head and mumbled to myself: "Praise be to Allah!"

Shortly after takeoff to the west, I could see the beautiful Pacific Ocean outside my window and the Santa Monica Pier in the near distance; I love the feel of taking off. It's a feeling I get inside that says I'm escaping from the everyday world to a destination where I'm a stranger to everyone. The pilot came on: "Lance, should be a smooth flight to Tampa with an on-time arrival. You have Sabirah and Rana at your service, so sit back, relax, and enjoy the three-and-a-half-hour flight."

I hadn't flown on a regular airline in so long I wouldn't know how to check in, let alone go through security with hundreds of people pulling out their toiletries in 3-ounce bottles; putting their laptops, iPads, or anything with an on/off switch in separate bins; then having someone barely educated with a G.E.D and attitude patting them down like they're all terrorists. No thank you. I like Clyde and the skinny lady in Hawthorne.

Ten

When I landed in Tampa, the humidity slapped me in the face so hard I thought I was a child again feeling my grandmother's backhand. Gladys Johnson didn't play. If you showed out back then, there was no child protective service coming to your rescue, no 911 operator to call. I was sweating just from the short walk from the jet to the private terminal. As soon as the sliding doors opened I felt the cool breeze from the air conditioner vent above the door. There was a short walk inside from the private terminal to the main terminal. I powered up my cell; I had two voicemails and a text message. I checked the text message first.

SMS—HI LANCE, ITS JORDAN, JUST WANTED TO SAY HI.

I didn't reply immediately, but I would later; business first. I checked the voicemails; one was from the store and the other was from a supplier. Both were non-urgent. As I came through the door of the main terminal, peace and quiet was instantly drowned out by crying babies, couples trying to find baggage claim, and airport announcements of gate assignments and arrival and departure time changes. I stopped by the main terminal restroom to drain the main vein. The in-flight asparagus made my urine stink a little. Nothing compared to the public urinal I was standing in front of. I always wondered, when you read the cleaning checklist on the walls of the bathroom what exactly are the employees checking off they've done? Exiting the men's room, my foot was nearly cut off by an old lady pushing a luggage cart not paying attention; damn, that hurt. As I approached the exit door of terminal A, a gentleman wearing TSA overalls walked as close as possible to me and slid a bulky manila envelope under my arm. When I met my good friend humidity again, I walked up the sidewalk and opened the envelope. Inside was a security company ID card, a car remote, cell phone, and a Bersa BP9CC handgun. Bersa was the finest in semi-automatic weapons made, in Argentina. I hit the car remote and the lights to a 2010 Dodge Challenger lit up. I started the American muscle machine and started my journey into Attorney Bach's world. The last time I was in Tampa was years ago for a football game and a shopping spree with Londen. Just outside of the Tampa Int'l Airport was an Embassy Suites hotel. I checked in and went up to my room. I unpacked my duffle bag and looked at the contents of a duffle bag from the Dodge Challenger. I had another Bersa, an extra shorty A2, hollow-point bullets, night goggles, a cryptic decoding device and twenty pounds of C4 explosives. I changed into a black jogging suit and headed to Cheval. The city of Tampa had grown a lot in ten years; new neighborhoods, new restaurants and stores, new outlet malls, and newly paved streets. The subdivision of Cheval was about an hour from the airport. Traffic was a little heavy but nothing compared to L.A. traffic. I stopped at a Starbucks on Dale Mabry and ordered a medium coffee with splenda. When I got to the gate of the Cheval subdivision, a guard came out with his clipboard.

"Good evening."

"Evening."

He took my badge looked at it. Turned it over and asked:

"New to the company?"

"I've been on for a month now, I normally work Steeple Chase. I think someone called in sick. I was asked to make the nightly run to Cheval."

"One minute."

The guard stepped back into his kiosk. I saw him on the phone. He didn't seem happy with the conversation on the phone. I had already chambered a round in the Bersa. I saw him write something on his clipboard as the conversation continued. His mannerism and body movement indicated one of two things: 1) the company didn't have me listed as an employee, or 2) he was upset he didn't get the chance to make some extra money. He hung up the phone. As he walked back towards the Challenger, I released the safety and placed the Bersa between my right leg and the middle console. I wasn't going to ask any questions or admit my guilt. Two rounds less and one less rent-a-cop would be the end-all. As the guard got closer, I adjusted my breathing so I wouldn't give away any signs of nervousness or wrongdoing. He walked up to the side of the car.

"Have a nice evening Mr. Clark" and handed my ID back and the gate into Attorney Bach's private world opened.

Driving through the subdivision to 7820 Canyon Ranch I took in the architecture of the million-dollar homes with privacy fences. The driveways were filled with luxury sedans, sports car, custom-made Harleys; not a Hybrid in sight. People on this level weren't avid supporters of the energy conservations. The checkbooks made the donation and paid for the research but their expensive taste didn't budge. Gas-guzzling and oil-company dividend returns was the name of the game around here. Attorney Bach was no different. As I slowly approached his mansion, I could see the well-manicured lawn and the exotic landscaping with the automatic sprinkler system. Outside his 4-car garage was a black Maybach he drove to work. The credit card imprint revealed that in addition to the German luxury, he had a custom restored '54 Chevy, a limited-edition Bulgatti Veyron and his wife drove the anniversary Range Rover. The twelve-foot windows were uncovered and inside I could see more elegant furnishings. As I drove past, my eyes instantly dilated from the high-beam bulb of a motion light. I parked a few houses down and pulled out the night-vision goggles to take a closer peek. In one room I saw who I assume was his wife talking to his daughter, the younger of his two children. His other daughter was 3 years older. In the kitchen I saw an older Cuban-looking woman cooking dinner. No sign of Phil. I

Empty Soul for Hire

looked at my watch—7:07 PM EST. He had to be home by now; Phil wasn't going to be easy. I pulled off and continued through the subdivision just in case the rent-a-cop up front had sent a second party to confirm my legitimacy. He seemed upset on the phone.

Driving back to Embassy Suites, my mind was busy trying to come up with a way to get to Attorney Bach. I knew my associates allowed me freedom to do my job, but soon they would want results. When I got back to my room, I turned on the television to SportsCenter. The NFL regular season was about to kick off and the Superbowl predictions were being talked about. Analysts said the Giants would be back, some were saying Mike Vick and the Eagles would make it this year but not to count out Ray Lewis' Ravens and the 49ers from out west would have to stand up to the Giants if they wanted a spot on the sidelines of the New Orleans Superdome. I thought about calling Jordan back but it was still early on the West Coast; my mind drifted back to the Arab flight attendant. I powered up my iPad and typed in www.eroz.com/tampa. This premiere escort website came alive midst the downtraughting economy. Hundreds of mommy and daddy's little princesses were online with erotic pictures and inviting profiles. Little princesses offering half hour to weekend time for reasonable gift amounts. The website wasn't shabby by any means and all major cities had an active part in this relaxing service. At your request, the woman of your choice would come to your specified location after a bite-size background check. You had two categories to choose from—independent and agencies. Any race, sexual preference, breast size, sexual experience was a small gift contribution and phone call away. Browsing the available outcalls in Tampa, I saw beautiful Ebonys, Latinas, Super Busty, Super Booty, European, GFE, BBW, and white females; all of them describing the fantasy of a lifetime, posing desirably, telling you their visiting dates, and smiling right at you. These women I'm sure had big dreams of being successful CEOs, accountants, bankers, investment brokers, happily married wives, heads of PTA boards but the good old U S of A had crushed them and left them this alternative. I looked in the Ebony folder but didn't see anyone that interested me. I looked in the European folder, but the pictures looked fake. A lot of females enhanced their photos. The mature folder looked better than I expected. These 40 to 50 year olds were beautiful with all medical receipts to support that beauty. I laughed to myself. I went back to the Ebony folder. There was a cute little twenty three year old Brazilian with sexy lips and hypnotic eyes (probably contacts), not that I was interviewing for beauty. In my current state I wanted to pay someone not for the pleasure but to leave after I was pleasured. An old Army buddy of mine used to tell his soldiers. "When traveling them streets, ain't no love out there. Leave the money by the bed and take the used condoms with you!" I wonder what Townsend is up to these days. We haven't spoken in years.

Her profile name was Carnival Cutie and the caption read *Let me bring the celebration to you.* I read her enticing profile and viewed the picture of her posing in lingerie, with gleaming white teeth and long eyelashes. Her skin looked flawless through the 4th Generation iPad, but what would she really look like when I opened my door? I picked up my cell and dialed the number. A professional voice answered on the second ring.

"May I help you?"

"Yes, I'm looking for Carnival Cutie."

"Is this a good call-back number?"

"Yes it is."

"Your name?"

"Call me The Visitor!"

"Real name Sir, or the call won't be returned."

"Lance Goodman"

"Mr. Goodman, your call will be returned within an hour if there's an available time slot."

"Thank you"

The call disconnected. The next call I made was to Jordan. I was a little apprehensive to return her call so soon because I didn't have time to go through the clandestine meet and greet with her. I knew she'd ask question after question. Working at the bank I was certain she had checked my account balance and bank activity. It was human nature to do such things when someone's on a first-name basis with one of the bank managers. I put my cell back on the nightstand and turned my attention back to the television. I browsed the guide to see what was coming on. The time change didn't really affect me too much unless there was a basketball game on west of the Mississippi. OKC was playing the Clippers on TNT at 10:30 EST. If my call wasn't returned I guess I would try to stay up and watch as much of the game as I could before falling asleep.

Eleven

The bank was closing shortly and I didn't have any plans this evening. I called and texted Lance but he hadn't returned eitherl. I guess he was busy at Kinkos assisting innovative pioneers with their designs and drafting plans. I'm not going to sweat the brother, but he is fine and appears to be legit and straight. The small seven-digit balance ain't bad either, and the address on file says he stays in Los Feliz Hills. He has to be buying, in that zip code there weren't too many rentals and those rentals had a numbered apartment or unit attached; his address didn't. I said my goodnights to the workers and night security of First Federal as I exited the building to catch the Blue Line home. Riding the train was always an adventure. You had routine riders like me and many other downtown workers. You had the lowlifes hopping on and off the different lines begging, with the same story. Then you had the tourists on vacation visiting the land of the celebrities and big lights. I used to laugh at them sitting or standing holding their maps and discussing their sightseeing ventures, never once thinking about getting mugged or robbed. I was interrupted from my people-watching when my phone rang blasting Ice Cube's "I got my loc's on." I didn't recognize the number so I answered professionally . . .

"Jordan Hughes."

"Hi Jordan, it's Khan."

"Hi Khan, how's it going?"

"It's good; wanted to see if you had plans tonight?"

"I was supposed to hook up with some girlfriends." I lied but I didn't want to seem like I led a boring life; his phone call was the first.

"Oh okay. Well if your plans fall through, hit me up."

"I will do that. Is this your cell?"

"Yes it is. By the way, have you worn the skirt and blouse?"

"Actually I haven't yet."

"Ok. Well I hope to hear back from soon."

"Alright. Have a good one."

And just like that I may have a date after all. I wasn't going to call him right away. When I got home I would check my mail, call Miriam, and watch my DVR recording of Oprah. Then if it wasn't too late I'd give Mr. Khan a call back to meet. But either way I'd call him. He sounded sexier on the phone than in person.

Twelve

The cell phone from the manila envelope I'd received at the airport buzzed on the nightstand. The phone number displayed didn't have an 813 Tampa area code and the phone was a fresh jump-off from my local contact. I answered rudely: "Yeah!"

"Is this Mr. Goodman?"

The sultry soft-spoken voice on the other end of the phone was Carnival Cutie.

"Speaking."

"I have an outcall timeslot available this evening; are you interested?"

"How long is the timeslot?"

"How long would you like?"

"All night and possibly the following evening"

"Mr. Goodman, let's start with a couple of hours and discuss all night once you know what gifts I like."

"I'm sure there's no gift I couldn't afford."

"What's your address?"

"I'm at the Embassy Suites on Westshore by the airport."

"What is your room number?"

"1211."

"I can be there in an hour."

"See you then."

"Mr. Goodman, are there any special request?"

"Like what?"

"GFE?"

"No thank you."

"One last thing Mr. Goodman."

"Yes?"

"I like my gifts upfront."

"I figured as much."

    When the telephone foreplay was done, I hopped in the shower and brushed my teeth. It didn't matter how many outcalls Carnival Cutie had before coming to my side of town, I knew she'd be Dove fresh and smelling expensive. I wanted to extend the same courtesy during my celebration. It hadn't been quite an hour and I heard a light tap on my suite door. When I looked through the peephole, I saw a woman standing about 5 ft 2 in, a light mocha complexion, long hair with a lightweight jacket on and a pair of black pumps. I opened the door and from her lips, the words flowed: "Mr. Goodman?"

"Last I checked. Can I take your coat?"

"Please."

She walked over to the table where the small gift was placed. She looked at the gift, turned around with a smile and said: "You have nice taste Mr. Goodman."

The nice taste she spoke of was $5000.

"Please call me Lance."

"Okay Lance."

She sat down on the sofa in the living room of my suite. I poured two glasses of wine and walked over to the sofa. She took a sip and smiled. In these situations it wasn't about getting to know one another or casual conversation. It was a win-win agreement between mutual parties. The parties both knew the terms, time limits, and boundaries that could and could not be crossed. She finished her glass of wine and asked if I had any music. I put my iPod on the docking station and found a playlist of R&B to play. After the music started she walked over to me and began massaging my shoulders. Her hands were soft but strong and felt good. She lifted my t-shirt over my head and untied my sweats. As she slid my sweats down, I noticed her checking out my manhood. When she came back up, she whispered in my ear: "Let's go to the bedroom."

She pulled out my manhood and began stroking him. Then she knelt down and started kissing around the tip of my manhood. Still stroking him she took him deep inside her wet mouth. Her strokes were in better rhythm than Fred Astaire. Carnival Cutie knew just how to get my manhood to new limits. He was nice and wet from her luscious lips and my moans started to get intense as she sucked deep, sucked slow, and massaged him intimately . . . . I heard her slurping on my man juices and my knees buckled slightly. She had my manhood blazing hot and firmly erect, I couldn't wait any longer.

I pulled her up and led her to the bed. As we climbed into the bed, I paused for a second or two admiring her youthful body. It was sexy, inviting, and well maintained. I slid the condom on and pulled her on top of me; my manhood was hard and erect. She enjoyed sliding my joystick inside her young hot and tight pussy and I easily obliged. It was something about the way she handled my manhood; it was well worth the gift I gave, better than any Black Friday holiday gift I had purchased. She was riding my manhood with a nice groove with her hands on my chest. I squeezed her young tender breasts with my hands and she moaned softly, playing her role like an academy award nominee. "Yes baby, that's it" she said. I began massaging her clit as she grinded her pussy on my manhood.

"Come on Carnival Cutie, where's the celebration you promised?"

"Yes Lance, your big stick feels good baby." More paid for lies.

"Yes your pussy feels so good and she's soaking wet too." I lied.

"Yes baby you got her wet, she's so wet Lance." More lies.

She closed her eyes and found that good spot and she rode my manhood hard and fierce. I felt her child bearing lips tighten around my manhood.

"Lance that's it baby, that's it, I'm coming baby, I'm coming."

I believed her; the condom was well lubricated from her release. I took her and flipped her over; her firm backside in the air. I wanted to go deep inside this young tender roni. I put my hands around her hips as I slid my hot manhood back inside. Her money maker was so wet that my joystick slid in easy and I began stroking one of Brazil's natives nice and strong. I pulled her hair, arching her back, and felt my manhood ease in a little deeper. I spanked her young tight bottom and ask her to lie to me "Is it good?" She lied in a soft moan voice "Yes Lance." As my manhood continued to slide in and out of her Brazilian pleasure zone, my breathing increased and my strokes got harder. We had been going for an hour, well within the price range of my gift. In one swift move she reached back and began squeezing my family jewels. I could tell she wasn't used to handling her client this way; at best most were old gents popping the blue or yellow pill and barely lasting twenty minutes. Not me! I knew how I wanted this night to go regardless of the gift required. I wasn't going to stop shopping until my gifts were well received, and I had expensive taste. I felt my volcanic eruption approaching and she must have as well. She began bouncing her ass faster against my strokes and our rhythm together was better than the battle of the bands between two HBCUs. The male reproductive cells inside me were ready to be released. Perhaps it was my short intense breaths or female intuition, but the gift recipient pulled away from me mid-stroke, pulled off the birthing conception preventer and sucked my manhood. With a few sucks and strokes, the Brazilian delight had swallowed a good amount of my unharvested seeds. My bloodline tree remained branchless and my Social Security number still free from the government child support system.

The young international liar lay asleep in my suite as I stood on the balcony smoking a Padron 1964 Maduro cigar thinking about Attorney Bach. He wasn't going to be an easy nab. His funding resources gave him a small sense of security. *DaCapn* would break through his lightweight firewalls and get my associates what they needed. I heard the sinful sheets on the bed moving around. When I turned around I saw the paid actress gather her things and head into the bathroom. I continued looking out into the Tampa/St. Pete Bay; the deadly humidity had gone to sleep but would return stronger than ever by early morning. I walked back into my suite and Carnival Cutie had showered and gotten dressed. I was confused because I thought I had given an expensive enough gift.

"I'm sorry Mr. Goodman."

My timeslot was over!

"Why?"

"I didn't come prepared for such an expensive gift."

"No problem. But normally refunds aren't an option."

"That is true."

"So what do you suggest?"

She stood there looking innocent like this was her first time receiving a gift. She batted her beautiful eyes and fidgeted trying to feel me out. I may have been a visitor in Tampa, but I wasn't a rookie to the gift exchange program. This gift exchange wasn't like the office Christmas party where somebody could steal your gift two times and shop it around for someone to get. This was a mano a mano arrangement and I wasn't exactly satisfied. I wanted the full value of my gift. I broke the silence,

"Carnival Cutie!"

"Yes Mr. Goodman."

"I have a suggestion."

"Yes."

"How old are you?"

I knew I was breaking the silent rules but I knew she would lie.

"I'm 23."

Maybe she didn't lie.

"Keep the gift and come back later on today."

I knew I was buzzing from the tobacco grown in the sunlight because no matter how sincere the conversation sounded and how firm we shook hands, when you closed your door from the outcall the deal was sealed and done. She looked at me, bashfully like a daughter looks at her father and politely said, "Okay I have your number."

Yes she did have my number and several others. Her mind had already decided what she was going to do with my gifts. Those thoughts didn't include coming back to Suite1211. My mind drifted to the Pacific Standard Time zone and wondered what Jordan was doing. I should have returned her call.

Thirteen

The alarm on my iPhone kept beeping every five minutes in between my snooze taps. My body time clock was still on Cali time and still recovering from my celebration the night before. I had to give credit where it was due and the young lady with the alias of Carnival Cutie lived up to every word of her online ad. Too bad you couldn't write reviews. LOL. I got up, looked outside my window and saw several metal objects with wings falling out of the sky. Weekly commuters and vacationers arriving into sweat city. When I got downstairs breakfast was almost over. The male waiter was nice and informed me if I wanted something from the grill, I should order in the next five minutes. I acted on his kind gesture and went straight to the grill. The chef was a heavyset man with a full beard. For a second I thought it was the rapper Ricky Rose back there scrambling eggs. I could tell he had a slight attitude when he looked at his watch.

"What we having this morning?"

"Do you have French toast?"

"We do, anything else?"

"Two scrambled eggs with cheese and ham steak."

"Coming right up Sir. I'll have it brought to your table."

"Thank you."

I pulled out my iPad and checked the NBA scores. OKC lost to the Clippers by 3 points. In the last few seconds Westbrook attempted a 3-pointer to tie and was unsuccessful. Not bad for a team that moved from San Diego and is sharing an arena with the Lakers. The Clippers were becoming the premier team in L.A. as the Lakers continue to build a team around this kid from Philadelphia. They weren't the Lakers of the '80s that had one of Michigan's finest, a center from UCLA, a strong forward from North Carolina, a shooting guard from Morningside High School in Inglewood, and Clark Kent. An older female waitress brought my order to the table and asked if I wanted more coffee. I declined but asked for some more water. The French toast made by Ricky Rose smelt good, the hint of cinnamon and powdered sugar present on each piece of the Texas toast. The ham steak was cured with maple brown sugar and the eggs were scrambled perfectly with cheese. I looked back at the kitchen as the chef was shutting it down and cleaning the grill. We made eye contact and I raised my coffee cup to him and nodded extending my appreciation for his skills. He returned the nod.

I gave the young male valet my ticket to have the Challenger brought around. When he pulled up, he jumped out energetic and said, "Nice car Sir."

"Thank you."

I gave him a tip and left the hotel. Driving through the city was nothing like my drive in L.A. The people weren't honking their horns every two minutes. You still had the ladies driving and putting on make-up, the men drinking coffee and trying to text or read emails from their smartphones. I guess that part of daily commuting was universal no matter what city you lived in. You could see the tall building of 100 North Tampa for miles. As I entered the downtown district, I took in the area to assess the one-way streets, which streets led directly to the I-75 and I-4, where the satellite police station was, how far was the bay, and how many traffic lights there were before I could be out of downtown. I found a parking garage two blocks from

Empty Soul for Hire

the tall building and parked. I stopped by a Starbucks and picked up some fruit and a bottle of water. You had to stay hydrated down here. I hadn't walked a quarter of mile and I could feel the sweat beading on my skin from my good friend humidity. The courtyard of the tall building had benches so I sat down and continued watching people walk to work and local vendors set up their kiosks to sell sundries to the employees of downtown Tampa and the vacationers. I didn't expect to see Attorney Bach for another hour. Sitting on the bench I took in the tall building. It had 18 floors with over a hundred offices, a lot of glass, six elevators, and security at the front door. I saw the black Maybach drive by and a black SUV behind it turn into the garage. I stood up and entered 100 North Tampa. The security inside had four men and a female. Two of the male security guards looked to be in good shape; possibly a challenge. The female guard was tall and thick, not fat though. She probably could hold her own. The other male security guard was basically biding his time until he could apply for Social Security. All of them except the older gentlemen had Glock 9 millimeters on their belts. When I walked up to the security station, the female guard greeted me.

"Good morning, what office are you visiting?"

"Harris, Architect and Engineering."

"Can I see a photo ID?"

I gave her the ID from the manila envelope.

"Okay Mr. Bickerman. We just need to look inside your briefcase."

"No problem."

I clicked the two locks on the Ferragamo leather case and turned it around for the female guard to view. Inside she physically saw drawings, a calculator, some pens, and more business cards with the name Bickerman. What this rent-a-cop couldn't see or feel was the Bersa encased in the bottom. They didn't have metal detectors or public humiliation screening like the airports across America had

Empty Soul for Hire

thanks to the 911 attacks. When she was done inspecting the leather case, she told me where the elevators were and wished me a good day. I wished her the same and put her in my mental database. I might have to put her on the payroll because I knew this job wasn't keeping her mortgage or rent paid and her nails manicured and who knew what other expensive habits she had. She could help with Attorney Bach. At the elevator, a nerdy, skinny man said good morning. I nodded. I was getting focused before getting to work. I knew I wasn't going to grab Phil without some collateral damage or worse, possibly a large count of dead bodies. When the elevator doors opened, the nerdy man and I entered. He pushed the 7th floor button and asked me which floor? I told him the 17th floor. He pushed my floor and the button to close the doors. The doors were almost closed when a polished brown loafer kept the doors from closing. It was my target, the man who was hiding witnesses. When the doors opened up, he stepped in and spoke to the nerdy man and me. He pressed the 18th floor button. He stood looking at his cell phone unconcerned that he was standing in the elevator next to the man that would take him, torture him, and finally kill him. The elevator reached the 7th floor and the nerdy man exited saying: "Have a good day Mr. Bach."

"You too, Mr. Williams."

The doors closed and my first thought was to push the emergency button and take Mr. Bach. I'm sure the elevators were on video at the security desk, so that wouldn't work. I could continue to the 18th floor with him and say the 17th floor was pushed by accident. His office occupied the entire 18th floor. That wouldn't work either. The elevator reached the 17th floor and the doors opened. I stood there momentarily. The doors were about to close. Mr. Bach pushed the button to hold the doors open and said: "Is this your floor?"

"Oh yes it is. Sorry I was daydreaming."

"I do that too sometime. Tell Ms. Harris I said Hello."

"Who?"

"Ms. Harris. She's the owner of the architect firm on this floor."

I was really not concerned about seeing Ms. Harris. My mind still had racing thoughts of how to grab his greedy pathetic ass right here and now. The elevator doors began to close and I said quickly: "I will tell her."

Mr. Bach was headed to the 18th floor; my chance of grabbing him had dematerialized right before my eyes. I turned around and walked to the uninteresting architect firm. My mind was consumed with the building drawings of 100 North Tampa and how I could get my hands on them. Suite 1700 was a nicely decorated office with metro furniture and bizarre paintings on the wall. The receptionist was an older lady with salt and pepper hair. She was still putting on her face when I walked through the door. She quickly closed her compact and politely as can be she gave me a warm welcome.

"Good morning Mr. Bickerman. Can I get you some coffee or tea?"

"Good morning. Some tea would be great."

The older lady stood up and walked to the nearby credenza where the keurig single cup making machine was. She turned around and told me the flavors of tea available. I asked for the green tea with a half pack of splenda. Sitting in the upscale architect office, I kept looking up at the ceiling to the 18th floor. The receptionist brought my green tea and told me Ms. Harris would be in shortly. I thanked her and sat back in the chair sipping my green tea. I pulled out my cell and checked my emails; nothing but spam and vendors soliciting to become Kinko suppliers. I looked up and Ms. Harris was walking through the frosted glass doors.

"Good morning Susan."

"Mr. Bickerman give me a few minutes and I'll be right with you."

She didn't give either of us time to respond and kept walking to her office. Susan smiled at me. Her smile told me she was used to the brash entrance and rhetorical greeting and not to take it personal. I nodded and kept drinking my tea and occasionally looking up at the 18th floor. Ms. Harris returned to the lobby, bubbly and all smiles.

"Mr. Bickerman, welcome."

I stood and extended my hand. She shook my hand very firmly and with direct eye contact. She stood about 5 ft 10 in, and had blonde hair, blue eyes, and the finest tan Florida sunshine could offer. I didn't see a ring on her commitment finger. I smiled and she told me to follow her to her office. As I walked by the receptionist, I thanked her again for the tea. Inside Ms. Harris' office on her walls I saw photographs of her standing in front of Big Ben in London, the Louvre in Paris, riding a camel somewhere in the middle east, standing in the white sands of the Caribbean islands and multiple photos standing with influential people. I noticed one in particular of her with the 18th floor occupant. They were at a black tie event, both showing pearly whites. I wondered how close she was to Phil. My mind had a help wanted sign plastered inside and I was becoming desperate for an employee or two to help me nab the high-profile attorney.

"So Mr. Bickerman, you're moving to Tampa and you want to custom build your home?"

"Yes ma'am and you come highly recommended."

"Please call me Kathy."

"Kathy it is."

"Did you bring the draft drawings?"

"I did. On the elevator up, a gentlemen going to the 18th floor told me tell you hello."

"Ahhh . . . Mr. Bach is a nice gentleman, and I normally don't like attorneys."

I didn't give a damn if he was nice or not. I'm sure he was quite the gentleman and family man. But his greed and disdain for protocol had pushed him into a league he wasn't ready for. At the moment I couldn't nab him from 100 North Tampa right away, but old man time was definitely on my side and running out on his.

"So you guys are colleagues?"

"We've been in this building the longest, and I see him at the gym sometimes."

"There's a gym in this building?"

"No. There's a Ballys a couple of blocks from here."

"Oh okay. I'll have to stop by after I leave here and check out the facilities."

"It's nice. They offer kickboxing, zumba, spinning, and have tons of free weights and machines."

"Thanks."

"Now let's take a look at these drawings. Do you know where you want to build?"

"I was hoping you could tell me some premier location with nice lot sizes?"

"Of course I can."

As Kathy rattled off several locations, my mind went back to Phil. It told me Ballys might be my only opportunity to grab him without the big crowd and security. I tuned back into the conversation to let Kathy know I was listening. She was a true professional and

Empty Soul for Hire

knew the Tampa area very well. She told me about the flood areas, hurricane evacuation areas, which insurance companies didn't write polices, and pricing per square foot. I didn't want to burst her bubble but she would probably see me once or twice more; if at all. My meeting with her was just to get a look inside 100 North Tampa without drawing attention to myself. I didn't want to be rude but it was time to move another chess piece in this expensive game and my opponent was on the 18th floor. After we finished the meeting, we stood and shook hands. Kathy told me she looked forward to working with me and would have her designers work on my drawings as soon as she received my initial deposit. My initial deposit would secure her firms services and she would file for the zoning and building permits with the county I chose to build in. She walked me back to the lobby and we said our goodbyes. Exiting the frost glass doors I walked up to the elevator and for a split second I thought about pushing the up button. My body must have had the same impulsive thought, because my finger moved uncontrollably. Before I knew it the up button had been pushed.

Fourteen

I didn't keep my word. I fell asleep watching my recording of Steve Harvey's new show. Talking about a success story, the man that did stand-up comedy, kept a perfect haircut, wore the dapper suits and flamboyant ties was now on radio and TV and had sold millions of copies of a relationship book. I will definitely call Mr. Khan today on my lunch break and see if he still wants to hook up. I checked my phone and I had a text message from Miriam and one from Lance.

SMS—Hi Jordan, sorry I didn't return your call or text sooner. I've been a little busy. Let's catch up soon though, Lance.

Well, it's about time Mr. Kinkos. If I hadn't heard back from him in couple of days I was going to toss his card and the next time he came to the bank it would be a strictly professional exchange—If I didn't shut my window down and take a break when I saw him next in line. I opened the blinds to see Mr. Sun stretching across the smog skies of my city. I put some water in my tea kettle and placed it on the front burner on low and jumped in the shower. As I showered and ran the loofa sponge across my body, my mind drifted and I thought to myself . . . *what's wrong with these men?* Look at me. I'm sexy, educated, child free, drama free, I have a job, and I'm damn near debt free. All I get is games, lies, and men still sucking on their mama's breast; selfishness and no sense of romance. I'm tired of having unfulfilled sex, laying there lying, telling a man it feels good when they're not hitting my spot or even coming close. Just basically humping on top of me or behind me with no rhythm, no swagger; another underachiever I let in between my legs. In the end, shortly after they left, I would open my nightstand drawer and pull out my toy of choice to make myself climax. I heard the tea kettle roaring from the heat underneath its bottom. I stepped out of the shower, walked to the kitchen and turned the water off. I poured a cup of tea. I walked into my room and looked in my closet to see what I would hit downtown L.A. and the brothers on the Blue Line with. I wanted to wear a dress but I wasn't sure of the temps and I didn't shave my legs in the shower. I wasn't a werewolf but I hadn't shaved my legs in a few days. Black slacks it is.

I stepped out of my condo and immediately felt good about the day ahead. The morning dew was a little cool. I threw my skull-candy earphones on and headed to the train. On the train, I sat pondering how I would come at Khan when I called him and whether I should call Lance back since he claimed to be so busy. There was a musty man standing next to my seat. I caught him trying to make contact when I looked up. He was really stinky. How did he get dressed this morning and not know he stunk.

"Hi!"

Really? He spoke to me? I ignored him.

"You could at least say hello." he continued.

"And you could at least shower and put on deodorant" I responded.

My stop was next thank God. I got off the train, gave Henry his $10, and made it to the bank. I walked in and cordially spoke to everyone before heading to the ladies room. In the ladies room I put on my M.A.C lipstick, looked in the mirror and adjusted my black La Perla undies before getting my day started. When the doors opened, an onslaught of customers stormed the lobby. I looked around the bank to see if there was a banner that said we were giving away money today. Maybe these people had hit the daily pick 3, pick 5 or the mega-millions lottery and were depositing what was left after Caesar aka IRS took a big portion. I wasn't ready to be this busy so early. My first customer had a bag full of rolled-up coins to deposit in his savings account. Another customer made a small withdrawal and the next few customers had similar transactions. I had to ask a coworker was the ATM down or something? When I took my lunch break I tried the ATM to see what the deal was; my $20 withdrawal came out with no problem. The ATM was working fine so I didn't understand the heavy traffic *inside* the bank. If that keeps me employed and off the pole I will keep a bright and shiny smile for the customers. I went to the Spanish truck parked on Grand and 9th. The line was long of course but worth the wait. It seemed like overnight these lunch trucks had taken over the lunchtime rush hour trade with their tasty authentic cuisines and reasonable prices. While standing in line, I pulled out my cell and sent Khan a text message.

SMS—Hi, sorry I didn't call you back last night. I'm on my lunch break; can you talk?

I was closer to the front and I could see the menu now. I had a taste for the chicken pita but the lamb smelt good this morning. Bob Marley rang out *"I shot the sheriff."* There was a text message from Khan.

SMS reply—Hi Jordan, nice to hear from you. What's up?

I ordered the lamb with rice and a pepper on the side, then called Khan.

"Hello."

"Hi Khan, how are you?"

"I'm well, what about you?"

"Great, just waiting on my lunch."

Empty Soul for Hire

"Sounds good. So what's up? Would you like to get together?"

Brother man sure didn't waste time getting to the point.

"What did you have in mind? Please don't say the movies."

He laughed.

"No I want to get to know you. Not sitting in a theater in silence and then talking about a movie. That's dumb."

He got some points for having a little dating sense.

"Some friends of mine are having a couples game night and I thought it would be cool, if you didn't mind."

"Okay. What kind of games? Taboo, Dirty Minds, games like that?"

"I believe those were the very games on the evite. Interested?"

I thought for a minute about the date proposal and whether it would be fun. Had he told his friends about me? Would they think we were a couple? How many other women had he extended the invite too? I wasn't telling him where I lived, so where were we meeting? My daydreaming was interrupted by the horn of a bus and Khan's voice calling my name.

"Sure I'd like to go. When is it, and I assume the dress is casual?"

"This coming Saturday from 7 until. They're having finger foods and drinks."

"Sounds good."

"Do you think we could meet for coffee or something before then?"

He was thinking the same thing I was thinking. A first date to see how we gel instead of showing up with a group of people not knowing anything but that he worked at Banana Republic and we met while I was shopping there. Speaking of Banana Republic,

"How often do you work at BR?"

"It's a part-time gig. I'm saving to buy a condo or a house if the rates stay low. I'm an elementary school teacher."

"Oh okay. It's nice to have goals. I'm sure you'll meet them."

"Trying hard, but sometimes after dealing with the children, the last thing on my mind is standing on my feet another six hours."

"I hear you. Keep it up and good luck."

"Thanks. So what day works for you for coffee?"

I didn't want him to think the most entertaining thing I did was watch DVR shows.

"Let me get back with you; I have a few things going on this week."

"No problem; just let me know."

"Good talking to you Khan."

"Likewise Ms. Jordan and I look forward to seeing you. Both times."

I finished my lunch and headed back to work. Walking through the front door I was about to clock back in when my cell phone rang. I looked at the screen and it displayed the word KINKO. I had given Lance that name in my contact list. I motioned to answer his call, excited to see KINKO on my screen. The phone rang again. I almost answered; I wanted to answer but I couldn't let him know I was excited. Besides, it took him a whole day and half to get back to me. The phone rang again.

"Hi Lance, what's up?"

Fifteen

I was standing by the counter with the deposit and withdrawal slips when this Hispanic man in his best English said, "cuse me ma'am, are you using this pen?"

My cell phone was no longer ringing but the screen now read 1 MISSED CALL and underneath was a picture of an envelope; I had a voicemail. I needed to get this day over. It wasn't normal for me to have date plans with one man and another man too busy to call blowing up my electronic device. KINKO would have to wait; Khan was now the leading candidate for the service mechanic position. When my day ended, I got on the train en route back to my lifeless existence and my most recent cable box recordings. I was excited about seeing Khan and the chance to hold a conversation with an attractive man with good sense who wasn't excited about the next video game release. The idea had me feeling positively capricious. I poured a glass of merlot and turned on the Wheel of Fortune. It was one of the longest running game show on and Pat Sajak and Vanna White still looked great. The contestants never lost their hunger for money, trips, and cars.

I relaxed for a few minutes, then I listened to my voicemail from Lance.

"Hi Jordan, I hope you're doing well. I apologize for not calling sooner but I have a new project that's keeping me busier than I expected. I will call you later or you can reach me on my cell."

The prerecorded voice on my cell told me I could save the message by pressing 9 or press 7 to delete. I pressed 7. I called Khan to set up our first meet-and-greet since the Banana Republic dressing room. The phone rang three times and he picked up. He sounded like he was working out or something because he was breathing heavy.

"What's up Jordan?"

"You tell me. Why you breathing like that? Were you busy?"

"I was doing Tae Bo."

"Billy Blanks?"

"Ha ha yes."

"You still have a VCR?"

"It's on DVD, silly. What's up?"

"I was calling to see if Wednesday works for you at the Starbucks in the California Plaza on Grand?"

"It's a date. What time?"

"Is 6 good?"

"See you at 6."

"Okay I'll let you go so you can *rewind* your Tae Bo tapes. LOL."

"You have jokes. It's a DVD."

"Right."

My first thought when he answered the phone was he had company and I was interrupting. If that was the case my buzz would have been instantly killed and the reality of L.A. men would register, making things clearer. That application is looking good Mr. Khan; let's see how the interview goes. I scrolled through my cell contacts to K and pressed KINKO once to prompt the call. I held the cell phone looking at those 5 letters, my finger rubbing back and forth across the green *SEND* button to activate the call. My screen light timed out. I pressed the *SEND* button softly to light my screen again but not activate the call. I thought about how genuine Lance sounded at my window inside the bank, his smile and his light brown eyes; his stalwart body holding my attention. Why did it take so long to return my call? I hit the *END* button clearing my screen and put my cell phone on the kitchen counter and got ready to relax for the evening and see what Oprah was talking about or what couple had the $750,000 budget to buy their first home in Orange County on HGTV.

Wednesday arrived and I was getting nervous about meeting Khan. Any other week, the days would be moving slow as molasses. Like a gentleman, he called around noon and confirmed the time and place. I watched the clock for the rest of the afternoon. I got two text messages; one from Miriam and one from KINKO. I replied to Miriam and told her I was meeting Khan for coffee and that we had a second date Saturday with some of his friends. She was happy for me and wished me luck. And she teased me about the service mechanic position being filled so soon and asked about Lance. I told her he called twice and sent a couple of text message but I hadn't returned his call. Miriam being Miriam got all up in my mix asking me what was the problem and going on about how attractive Lance was. The truth is I was upset he didn't respond sooner. No matter how strong I looked at work, my self-confidence was on a low level and right now Khan was just the boost I needed. I told Miriam we'll see what happens. Besides, I wasn't meeting Khan with a wedding coordinator; it was for coffee.

The sun started to hide behind the tall buildings of Central L.A. as I sat by a window in the plaza waiting, I saw Khan walking towards the plaza. He was dressed in brown slacks and a light blue patterned shirt with a lightweight jacket on and a tote bag across his shoulders. His walk had some swagger to it, similar to that chocolate brother from the movie "The Cave." Khan saw me through the tinted glass and smiled. When he approached, he looked taller than I remembered. He smiled and came in for a hug. I hesitantly came in to meet his embrace; I didn't want him thinking it was that type of party. I would have preferred a handshake. These days you had to let men know upfront that you weren't a low self-esteem female willing to lay down with them just because they were hot and had a little money. He put his tote bag down and sat next me and said: "That wasn't too bad was it?"

"What?"

"The hug. I wasn't sure if I should extend my hand or my arms."

"The hand would have been better."

"LOL, noted Ms. Jordan. How was your day?"

"Not too bad, a normal day in the bank. What about you?"

"It was okay, starting to prepare report cards and get ready for parent-teacher night."

"Easy for you I'm sure."

"Are you kidding? Every parent comes to the meeting with an attitude and internal guilt."

"Internal guilt?"

"Yes. Their kids aren't getting C's and D's because of me. Those grades reflect lack of attention at home."

"Oh."

"But I want to know all about Ms. Jordan Hughes, her likes and dislikes."

"You make it seem like I have a printed out profile ready for you to review."

We both laughed. I suggested ordering something to drink; this interaction felt more like an interview than a date. He left his coat over our two seats and we got in line to order our expensive roasted brews with foam. As we walked by the free wireless intruders sipping their lattes and flavored teas back to our seats I felt Khan's hand in the small of back. If a handshake would have been better than a hug, why did this jughead think he could put his hand in the small of my back? I didn't make a scene but any more inappropriate moves or touches and this date would be cut short and he'd have to find someone else for game night with his friends.

Sixteen

When the modern day lift stopped on the 17th floor, the doors opened for the continued journey to the 18th floor. I stood there thinking about Phil Bach and how risky it would be to try and grab him now. I wasn't the afternoon shoot-out at the O.K. Corral type. I like minimal damage and few if any witnesses. Without a doubt, I could take out the minimum-wage security on the ground floor. But where was Phil's security team? The elevator doors began to close. I stuck my foot in between them to keep them from closing; they re-opened and I stepped in. My mind was working overtime as I stared at the buttons contemplating which one to push. The time wasn't right. I had to accept that and come up with another plan quickly. The lift doors began to close and I heard the voice of Kathy Harris, the architect say:

"Mr. Bickerman!"

I pushed the button to open the doors of the lift.

"Yes?"

"If your schedule is open around one o'clock, I'm going to Ballys for a kickboxing class. You can check out the facilities on one of my buddy passes if you like."

"I do have another appointment this afternoon. Let me see if I can change it. Can you leave the pass at the front counter?"

"Sure."

"Thank you."

I pushed the close door button of the elevator, still not accepting the present circumstances. I didn't push the ground floor button. I let the doors close and the lift remained on 17. After a few seconds the elevator began to descend on its own. Standing inside the mirrored elevator I wondered what security was thinking as they spied on me. What would be waiting for me on the ground floor? I heard a beep as the elevator passed each floor, continuing its descent. When the doors opened on the ground floor I didn't walk out immediately. I put my leather bag in position in case I needed to pull out the exotic Argentina peacemaker. As I proceeded through the lobby to the exit, I noticed the security guards talking amongst themselves about boxing and how some Asian guy and some guy from Detroit need to get it on. The conversation was loud as the guards shared their meaningless comments about each fighter. I knew who they were talking about. The buzz around the boxing community was that one boxer was dodging a specific drug testing method; while the other wanted too much of the fight purse. Either way boxing fans were left to wait impatiently while the two boxers continued beating a series of washed up, non-contenders. As I got to the exit, one of the guards stepped away from the conversation to wish me a good day. I didn't acknowledge his insincere wishes as I pushed the door instantly re-acquainted with my good friend humidity.

I checked my cell phone for messages that came in while I was meeting with the architect. I had two missed calls from last night's gift recipient, but she didn't leave a voicemail. Those weren't the calls I was hoping for. Jordan hadn't returned my call or replied to my text messages. I must admit I was surprised to see the missed calls from Carnival Cutie; for sure I wasn't the only gift giver passing through escaping spiritless sex between husband and wife. Why was she calling? Surely, in her line of work it wasn't to offer me a new customer freebie. I didn't return the missed calls. I walked around the downtown area spotting potential dead ends and ways to get to the highway quickly. A lot of one-way streets and small side alleys made it difficult to map out a solid plan. Collateral damage was going to be high no matter what. I looked at my watch—12:07 PM EST. Did I really feel like working out today or pretending to be interest in a gym membership? I headed to the parking garage to get my duffle bag. As I passed back by the eighteen-floor building, I saw the biracial high-profile attorney walking through the courtyard alone. I went inside my black leather case, pulled out the foreign hardware and chambered a round. My kidnapping thoughts were quickly interrupted when two of Phil's henchmen appeared in my view. Phil continued walking in the city's unfriendly evaporation northbound. I didn't know the city so I couldn't assume where he might be headed nor could I get in a midday shootout in a city where my resources were limited. I continued to the parking garage.

After I got my duffle bag I went to Bally's. It was a few minutes after one o'clock; hopefully my prospective designer was still there and had left the pass at the front desk. When I walked into the downtown social meeting spot I was greeted by another well-tanned woman sporting a fitness bra and tight gym leggings.

"Welcome to Bally's." she said.

"Hi, Kathy Harris left a pass for me."

"Let me check. What's the name?"

"Bickerman."

"Yes sir, here's your pass. Do you have any questions about Bally's?"

"Where's the men's locker room?"

The Barbie model pointed me in the direction of the men's locker room. I thanked her and proceeded to the naked walking lounge. The lounge had red lockers, four-foot benches, and carpeting. I saw the shower area off to the right with sinks and a medium-size wooden room, probably a sauna or steam room. What caught my attention though, was the iniquitous attorney getting undressed at a nearby locker. I quickly scanned for any naked walkers and more especially his trigger-ready henchmen. I heard a toilet flush and two shower heads from the shower bay. Without any further hesitation I pulled out the first thing with a handle on it from my duffle bag and some zip ties. Within seconds I was in front of Phillip Bach's half-naked body. When he turned around I had a foreign-made 9 mm pointed center mass and told him: "If you ever want to see your wife or daughters again don't move."

His eyes and mouth wide open, he finally said: "Can I at least get dressed?"

"Put your shirt back on; that's it."

I knew his henchmen weren't far away and if he wasn't out of the musty room soon they would be in to check on the pretty boy. I zip tied his wrists and we moved towards one of the emergency exits. After two or three steps, Phil shoved me into one of the lockers and tried to run. I tackled him to the ground and hit him in his ribs. We had to move quickly before the other patrons of the lounge came in. I picked him up and gave him another warning.

"Try that again and your daughters won't be at their pretty little private school waiting for your Sally homemaker wife."

He coughed trying to make enough noise for someone to hear him. I punched him again, this time in his stomach. We made it to the emergency exit and in his pathetic voice Phil asked: "Are you sure you know what you're doing?"

"I know exactly what I'm doing."

"My friends are going to come after me if I'm not in the free weight area in five minutes."

Empty Soul for Hire

"Five minutes is a lot of time; now shut up."

Outside Bally's we made our way back to the parking garage trying to go unnoticed as much as possible. I saw Phil looking around as we walked the short distance. He didn't make any noises or outcries. He was an arrogant prick. Before we got to the parking garage, I heard the sounds of brakes and horns nearby. I looked back and saw the two henchmen running towards us with their weapons drawn. One of the men was on a radio. I assume calling for more help to rescue the low life now in my possession.

"You certain you want to go through with this?" he asked.

His arrogance pissed me off.

"I'm more than certain."

I elbowed him in his side once more. I hit the remote to the Challenger and threw Phil in the front seat. As I buckled him in, I heard bullets coming my way. I returned fire from my foreign weapon. My bullets were more damaging than what I heard hitting the ground. Inside the Challenger, I shifted the gear to the D position and sped in the direction of fire. I knew his henchmen wouldn't keep firing in fear of hitting my passenger; at least they wouldn't keep firing at me. The back right tire of the Challenger burst as one of the henchmen's bullets hit it. The flat tire made me swerve on the downtown street as I floored the American muscle. I saw the red light ahead at the intersection on Zack but I kept my foot pressed to floor. I had to make it to I-275. The henchmen weren't far behind. I heard more brakes and more horns and nearly got hit by the on-coming green light traffic. Phil sat in the passenger seat silent, occasionally looking in the side mirror for his rescue team. The traffic light ahead on Tyler was green; I had a few more streets before I would reach the on ramp to I-275. Just as I got to Tyler, the light turned yellow. I kept up my speed and entered the intersection, risking another collision. One driver hit his brake and yelled obscenities as I sped through. I could see the interstate and the signs indicating I-275 ahead. My cell phone vibrated. I looked at the display; it was Jordan. I let the call go to voicemail. Speeding towards the multi-lane expressway, I didn't see the black Lincoln town car in my peripheral until it slammed into the back right side of my getaway car. Phil and I spun 180 degrees and I was face-to-face with the driver of the town car. I unloaded the Bersa through his front windshield. I saw his head snap back and the color of bright red splash across the glass. I knew there was more than one person in that vehicle. I unloaded the empty clip and loaded another fifteen rounds, my getaway car idling in drive. I waited to see who would exit the rescue car. The back doors of the town car opened and I saw one of Phil's saviors get out firing his weapon, I squeezed the trigger and the foreign peacemaker spit fifteen hollow points in his direction. Four rounds hit him; one to his left shoulder, one to his chest, and two to his right leg. He fell to the ground and grabbed his shoulder. Phil looked at me like a little kid witnessing his first scary movie. I didn't give in to his bewilderment; my eyes were on the town car. The man on the ground was still breathing as he put a radio to his mouth. I saw him moving his lips so I aimed my gun and fired at him. His skull split open and the uneducated brain matter spilled onto the Tampa neighborhood street. I took my foot off the brake and sped off towards I-275. I saw nosey citizens running towards the fender bender hoping to get their fifteen seconds of fame after the police arrived followed by reporters for the evening news.

Entering the on ramp of I-275, I slowed my speed to avoid waking up a highway patrol from a nap or donut break. It would be hard to explain why I had an influential attorney zip-tied in my front seat. Traveling north, I drove the speed limit and I pulled out the cell phone from the manila envelope I had received at the airport and pressed the send button by the second contact in the phone. After two rings, the voice on the other end answered and asked my ETA. I said thirty minutes. I saw Phil looking at me hoping I'd say a name or give any clue to help his pathetic self. He probably thought I was an amateur trying to strike it rich by kidnapping him. Driving to my undisclosed location, I saw two cars in my rearview mirror changing lane frantically and gaining speed. Phil must have seen the rescue pursuit because he looked at me and smiled. I held the steering wheel with my left and punched his annoying ass with my right hand. His head swung towards the passenger door and blood came out of his mouth. The rescue crew was two cars back now. Where is the highway patrol when you need them? One of the cars was coming up on my left and the driver slammed into the side of the American muscle—no respect for fine automobiles. The driver slammed into me and Phil again; my body jerked and I felt a slight ache. I made eye contact with the driver as he continued slamming into my getaway car. I was able to pull my gun out but I couldn't chamber a round because the driver kept slamming into me. Phil surprised me when he knocked the gun onto the floor board. I punched him again—twice this time. I slammed on the brakes to give me a few seconds to get my gun off the floor board. I chambered a round and released the safety. Now I was pursuing the rescue car. I sped up to the vehicle ahead and once I was close enough I started squeezing the trigger. The back window shattered and the driver swerved into another lane. Shots continued to hit the vehicle that was trying to rescue my passenger. If I had counted correctly I had three bullets left before I would have to load another clip. I put the gun between my legs and tried to catch up to the irritating driver and end this immature road rage. The second vehicle was not far behind now and my exit was close. I was side by side with the car that had played bumper cars with me a few miles back. He looked at me and said some vulgar words. I pulled my gun from between my legs and shot him in the side of his head. The car swerved to the left and hit the concrete barrier and flipped a couple of times. I saw the flames burst up into the sky through my rearview mirror. I heard some broken English from my passenger: "What do you want with me?"

"A few answers to some questions."

"You couldn't make an appointment?"

"No! My questions are little more complex than the standard law firm form you fill out in the lobby."

"OIC! And what do these questions pertain to?"

"I'll give you one guess."

Seventeen

Khan was a bold gentleman at heart. Maybe I was little paranoid from dating so many boneheads that I was overreacting. After we sat back down he and I talked about our careers more and some likes and dislikes. Turns out Khan moved here from Texas when he started high school and went to Pepperdine University for college. He told me he had been in a committed relationship with a young lady that had a kid. The relationship began to go sour when he made comments about her parenting techniques. He told me the arguing started small then eventually escalated and strained their relationship. I knew a little about his pain as I too, dated a guy with a little boy. The guy wasn't consistent and I tried telling him that children may not comprehend what adults tell them but they definitely imitate what they see. One minute he was trying to be Cliff Huxtable and the next minute he was the South Central gangster dad. Hell, I got confused sometimes. I told Khan about my dating nightmares, how I got into banking and what my long-term goals were.

I felt comfortable talking to Khan. He was a great listener and didn't brag too much about himself like most of the dudes in L.A. The conversation was going so well we lost track of the time. I had to make it to the train station and I normally don't catch the train this late; so who knows what crowd would be on the Blue Line. I stood to put my jacket on and Khan grabbed it to assist me.

"What garage are you parked in? I will walk you to your car."

"I catch the Blue Line train."

"It's kind of late; would you like me to take you to your stop where your car is parked?"

The idea sounded good but I didn't know him or if he was telling the truth about anything he said tonight. He could be a serial killer hiding behind his teaching job.

"No thank you. I will be okay."

"Jordan this is L.A.; I really don't mind."

"I don't know you. We just had coffee and told some stories."

"Girl, you are funny."

"No pun, but I do watch the news and all the criminal shows. LOL"

"Okay, have a good night and we're still on for Saturday. Right?"

"Khan, I'm going to trust you. You can take me to the parking lot at my stop."

You really can't be too careful these days but it was something about Khan that made me feel comfortable. When we got outside, he pointed in the direction of the parking garage where he was parked. As we walked towards the garage, we didn't hold hands and Khan didn't force anything. The city of angels was coming alive and the cool breeze felt relaxing. When we got to his car he opened my door like a gentleman. I reached over the middle console and opened his door.

"Thanks."

"You welcome."

"You don't find many old school women in this superficial city."

"You don't find many old school men in this shallow city."

"You're going to be good at game night."

"You're funny."

"So where are you parked?"

"At the Florence stop near Graham."

"Okay."

I wasn't expecting to walk up to the German precision maker. Khan drove an E350 Mercedes with the factory option. He hadn't sold his soul to one of the rim shops and destroyed the elegance of Mercedes. His radio was preset on the smooth jazz station. I noticed how he handled traffic and the impatient drivers. His demeanor was calm and collected. This brother was either acting real well or he really had his life together and knew what he wanted out of life. A rare thing in this fast, let's get in your panties world we lived in. Driving to the metro parking lot, the conversation was minimal since we talked so much over coffee. I didn't want to be too nosey but I asked: "How close are you to buying your first home?"

"I'm pretty close."

"I apologize for invading your privacy."

"No problem. We're getting to know each other, right?"

"Oh okay, good luck with your search. Are you preapproved?"

"My, my, now you're asking personal questions."

"I was just asking because my bank has some great rates. Calm down"

"Whatever! A lot of banks and credit unions have great rates these days."

"LOL."

When I got in my car I checked my cell phone messages. I had four messages from Miriam. All four messages said the same thing. How was my date going? Did she think I was going to text her while I was on a date? I love my girl but sometimes she's a little over the top. I didn't reply to her messages or call her. I wanted to get home, shower, and get ready for bed. I didn't hang out this late during the week. After my shower I turned on my tea kettle and made a hot cup of tea. Sitting in my bed I turned on the TV to catch an episode of the new Family Feud. That comedian turned author was the new host, he was everywhere. My phone buzzed. I looked at the screen and the name displayed was Khan's.

"Hello."

"Hi Jordan, I was calling to see if you made it home in one piece."

"I did thanks. I was just getting ready to turn in after some tea."

"I won't keep you. Thanks for meeting me this evening."

"I had a nice time and I'm looking forward to Saturday."

Oh my God why did I just say that?

"Have a good night."

"Good night Khan."

I laid in bed watching the two families answer the top four answers on the board. My mind was definitely on Khan and how we hit it off. I thought about KINKO as well though. Maybe I'll call him tomorrow on my break or lunch. I didn't know what I'd say to him without sounding disappointed or giving him attitude because of his rudeness. As I continued sipping my hot tea my eyes became tired. I set the sleep timer on the TV and nestled under the covers. The last thing I remember was the points were tripled for the top 3 answers on the board. The question was name a type of medicine your spouse would be embarrassed of if you caught them taking it? I heard someone blurt out Viagra but I don't remember which family made it to 300 points first. I dozed off when I heard a contestant say,

"We're going to play, Steve."

Eighteen

The second car bumped the side of the Challenger and I swerved into another lane coming close to the median barrier. I regained control of the muscle car and sped up. The rescue team for Phil was determined I had to give them that but my patience was running thin with the amateurs. My exit was coming up and I needed to end this re-enactment of the Orenthal James freeway chase. I didn't have a loyal sidekick with me; instead I had a grumbling attorney zip-tied holding on to his last hope of escape—the second car playing bumper cars with me. I heard the bullets hit the manufactured metal. I saw Phil duck down. The cavalry must have grown impatient since they were firing at the getaway car with their highly paid employer. The attorney made a comment to deaf ears—don't shoot at the car you idiots. I laughed. Up ahead I saw a sign saying my exit was 1½ miles ahead. I had to do something promptly and my options were restricted. I sped up to get some space between myself and the car chasing me; when I felt I could pull out the A2 semi-automatic weapon I slammed on the brakes and made a hard turn to the left so I was facing the oncoming traffic. I could see the driver gaining speed towards me. I got out of my car with the automatic weapon and began unloading shells on the expressway. The first shots hit the headlights and the hood of the car. The driver swerved but still headed my way without hesitation. I had his employer and the future of his retirement, and his family's well-being in my possession. A few bullets didn't shock him in the least. I continued firing, hitting the side mirror and side panel on the driver's side. Bullets sprayed the front windshield and the driver lost control of the vehicle. The vehicle slammed into the median and the hood caught fire. I ran to the vehicle to make sure the driver wasn't breathing. I saw him reaching for a radio. He looked up at me standing over him and said:

"You won't get away with this."

I heard a voice asking his location and if Phil was still alive. I raised my weapon and aimed it at him. I unloaded three shots center mass and one shot to the head. I came closer to the lifeless body and picked up the radio. I squeezed the talk button and told the other end: "Phil is alive at the moment but his life clock is ticking."

I turned around and I could see the attorney trying to escape the getaway car. I dropped the radio and started running towards him. He saw me running and amplified his escape attempt. I was ten feet away when he managed to get the passenger door open. I fired a shot from my 9mm to get his attention. He stopped moving and looked at me. I kept the gun pointed at him to convince him I would fire again if I had to. I wouldn't kill him but the torture and pain would begin sooner than later. In his pathetic voice he asked: "Who are you and who sent you?"

"Don't play coy with me. Get back in the car."

I waved the gun towards the car to let him know I meant right now, not when he felt like it.

"What do you want?"

"Shut your mouth. You will have plenty of time, well not plenty but you'll have a chance to speak."

"Speak about what?"

I punched him in his clean-shaven jaw.

Empty Soul for Hire

"Now sit there and be quiet."

I buckled his seat belt, blindfolded him, and took a survey of the expressway. All traffic had come to a halt. The fame seekers had their cell phones out recording the catastrophe in the middle of the busy commuter expressway. I had to get out of the public eye; this wasn't the time for a photo op. I got back in the car and threw the 307 horsepower transmission in D and made my way to Phil's new humble abode.

When we pulled up to the place where Phil would take his last breath, I looked around to see if we were followed by any last attempt rescue teams. The Challenger had taken a beaten from bullet holes and rounds of bumper cars from the steroid pushers trying to save their employer. But the engine still roared loudly, all 307 horses still intact if I needed to make another run. I parked behind the decrepit house and took my passenger inside. When I took the blindfold off, Phil looked around the room. No one was there but him and I.

"Not quite the plush living you're used to?"

"That's putting it mildly."

I began unpacking my duffle bag of goodies for Attorney Bach. How tasty the goodies would be depended on his timely or untimely responses. I'm not going to waste too much time; hell I'm tired and I know my associates are impatiently waiting for answers. I turned around to see the high-profile attorney sweating profusely with his head down. I slapped his face and he looked up but didn't say anything. I could see the exhaustion on his face. His daily routine had been abruptly interrupted; no lattes, he missed his workout and hadn't spoken to any of his colleagues, wife, etc. I felt no pity for him as I slapped his smooth face again. I gave him a few sips of water and began the timer to his last words.

"Now Phil are you going to tell me what I need to know?"

"What might that be?"

"Banderas"

"Who?"

"Banderas. Isn't he a client of yours?"

"I don't know what you're talking about."

"You don't?"

"No."

"Are you sure?"

"Yes."

With a pair of brass knuckles I punched him on his right temple; the skin of his well-groomed face opened slightly and blood slowly began running down his stubble face. I grabbed his face.

"Stop playing games Phil, you know exactly who Banderas is." He wiggled away from my grip and looked intently at me as if that would convince me he was telling the truth. I wasn't convinced. I grabbed the Tampa Herald newspaper and read the headlines to him: Attorney Bach continues to seek the release of Colombian drug lord Banderas. To date all bond requests have been denied as Banderas is a serious flight risk, etc, etc, etc. I slapped his face with the paper and asked again: "Banderas"

He fumed.

"Banderas, Phil?"

Silence

I grabbed the nearby bucket of cold water and threw it in his face and ripped his tailor-made shirt open and punched him in the chest. He coughed. I punched him again. In between punches and coughs he managed to say something: "Okay, okay. What do you want to know?"

"You know Banderas now?"

He spit again and tried with all of his might to get free from the chair. His legs were taped tightly to the legs of the chair and his hands were zip-tied behind his back against the chair. He almost tipped himself over and said: "What do you want to know about Banderas? Other than I'm filing appeals on his behalf."

"No you're not, Phil."

"Yes I am, I just filed another one last week."

"Is that right?"

"Listen, whoever you are, you need to speak to Banderas' associates about all of this."

"I have and they're onto your empty promises. Where are the witnesses?"

Phil laughed as if he couldn't believe I had so much information

"What witnesses?"

"You don't know about the witnesses?"

"Sir, you really have some bad information on Banderas' case."

"No, I'm certain of the information I've received. Are you saying you don't know about the witnesses?"

"That's correct."

I stood in front of the attorney clapping my hands applauding his resistance to give me the answers I wanted. The meeting in San

Pedro must be a mega merger in the making for him to continue lying in his current state. I left him alone in the room and went to the kitchen. I heated the front burner on the stove and sat a pair of vise grips on the fire. Once the metal teeth of the grips were blazing hot, with a pair of gloves I removed the tool from the fire and headed back to the meeting with Phil. He must have smelled the hot metal in the room because he started squirming crazily trying to get free. His efforts were unsuccessful. I pulled up a chair and sat in front of him. I returned the intent look he gave me earlier. He looked scared by the pair of hot vise grips. I gave him a grimacing smile and winked, then I reached behind the chair.

"Witnesses, Attorney Bach?" I asked.

He blinked his eyes a few quick times and looked around the room, still trying to free himself.

"Stop moving; you need all of your strength."

I squeezed the hot metal grips around his index finger and he screamed out for his spiritual maker. My ears were deaf to his request and I didn't release his finger right away. I could see his manicured finger turning blistering red then a shade of black. I felt no remorse for his pitiful rich ass.

"Witnesses, Attorney Bach" I repeated.

He was fuming and breathing heavily but didn't respond. I grabbed his middle finger and clamped the hot grips tightly as I looked at him close his eyes and tremble in agonizing pain. I came to the side of his face and said: "Come on, is it really worth all of this?"

He spit out vulgarities and told me I would pay for this. I let what he said resonate in my mind. He was right, the longer I wasted time on him, the more my opportunity faded with Jordan. Something about that young lady sparked my interest and I wanted to get to know her. She seemed very pleasant during our brief business exchange. I couldn't kill him yet though, I needed the locations of the witnesses first. I released the grips from his middle finger. I heard Phil exhale from the momentary break of pain.

"Think about your wife and daughters."

The mentioning of his family got his attention

"How do you know about my family? Who the hell are you?"

"Who I am should be the least of your concerns. Tell me where the witnesses are."

"I don't know about any damn witnesses."

His thoughtless and continued lies further pissed me off. I knelt down in front of him and untied his fancy loafers and pulled off his gold-toe black socks. He wiggled his toes and enjoyed the air and freedom. Unfortunately he wasn't getting a deluxe pedicure. Instead we were going to play the old game this little piggy went to the market. I reached inside my duffle bag and pulled out a heavy duty construction hammer. I saw his eyes grow big as grapefruits and he began shaking in the chair.

"Your wife and daughters?" I asked.

No response. I lifted the hammer and slammed it into his big toe, breaking the proximal phalanx of his big toe nearest the first metatarsal, and the distal phalanx of the big toe. The second toe containing three of the twenty six bones was crushed by the repeated hammer blows. His screams were so loud. The loudness of his screams were numb to my ears as each of his dainty remaining toes were crushed like ice. I needed answers not prayer request and repentance. I continued slamming the hammer until his right foot looked like the Playdoh kids played with back in the day. I had worked up a sweat dealing with his lies. I stood up and wiped my brow. Phil was crying now and the stink of urine was in the air. I inhaled the sweet smell and painful cries of my work. I looked at the man of criminal valor as he sat there in pain. I had no regards for his family, only thoughts of his greediness.

"Have it your way but, this is only the beginning."

He had enough strength to say: "Believe me, I don't know what you're talking about."

"Phil, tell me something. What was the meeting in San Pedro about?" I asked.

His heavy breathing stopped as if he had just caught his second wind. He looked at me with dark eyes in disbelief of the information I knew about him. His mind was tracing back over the tracks he thought were so well covered. I walked away and left him in the room alone. I stepped outside to contact my associates.

SMS—can you talk?

SMS reply—yes.

SMS—calling from an 813 area code.

SMS reply—okay.

A husky voice answered on the third ring and asked, "Where are the witnesses?"

"I don't know yet. He's holding onto their location."

"No slight sign of surrender?"

"I've punched him, crushed two of his fingers with hot vise grips, and broke every bone in his right foot."

"Turn up the heat. We need that information sooner rather than later."

Empty Soul for Hire

"How steamy do I need to get?"

"Until the location of the witnesses is given, light his greedy ass up. If he still resists, bring his children into the picture."

"His children?"

"Is the connection bad? His children."

"Okay, as you wish."

"I'll be in touch."

The husky voice disconnected. I stayed outside looking up at the stars. I never involved children or killed children directly. I'm sure the many bodies buried thanks to me had left behind a wife, child, or children. At my age, it was hard to believe that my tree of life was branch free. My tree saw one season year round, Fall. My bloodline remained singular with no son to carry my name forth, no daughter to walk down the aisle in front of family and friends. If someone went to that ancestry website to look me up, my trail would be so short they could play a longer game of hopscotch on the sidewalk. The rage in my blood mixed with the emotional dysfunction of letting anyone get close to me and committed kept my unfed appetite longing for its next prey and not birthday parties at Chuck E. Cheese, daycares, or potty-training. I was either tired from the day's event or I was becoming sentimental. I cracked my neck and jogged in place for a few minutes to regain focus on what I was hired to do. Emotions had no place in this line of work and I needed to remember I wasn't at Kinkos helping the pipe dreamers. In the distance, I saw headlights blaring in the direction of the house. I stayed outside to confirm their destination. In this economy it wouldn't surprise me if one of the fame seekers back on the expressway had taken money from one of Phil's goons. The headlights got closer;, the vehicle didn't slow down as it approached the house. The headlights didn't turn towards me. There wouldn't be another exchange of gunfire. I waited until I couldn't see the brake lights any longer then went back inside. When I returned, Phil was asleep in the chair, exhausted by our encounter.

It was not exactly the comfy bed he normally slept in, tucked away in his plush subdivision. I didn't wake him. He would need his strength in the morning. By noon, I would know the location of the witnesses or he'd be begging me to kill him.

Nineteen

I couldn't believe it was Saturday already. Khan and I had spoken a couple of times over the telephone and via text message since our first meeting. He wasn't aggressive and his timing was perfect. The phone conversation was casual but he asked relevant questions that kept me intrigued about him and where this thing might be going. I couldn't give away my treats too soon; but the brother's voice was intoxicating and he spoke intelligently. The conversation wasn't about him or his day; he asked about my day and how my metro ride was. He threw subtle hints of jealousy, asking how many customers tried to hit on me. His approach was indeed uncommon in this day and age. Most guys had the standard dialogue—*What's up; When we goin' hook up; Want some company tonight*? The change was gracefully welcomed. I finally returned Miriam's call and told her about the first date but didn't give her all the details. I kept it general. I had to with Miriam, or she'd swear I was sleeping with him and calling him my man. It didn't matter that she and Scott had been dating off and on for God's know how many years. I lost count after the last breakup, move out and move back in episode. I pulled out my cell—no missed calls or text messages from KINKO. I scrolled through the contacts to the K's and pushed the button to begin typing a message, but I stopped. What am I doing? This man hasn't talked to me since the bank. He sent a simple text message about being busy, blah, blah, blah, and I hadn't heard back from him. I guess he thought I would be ringing his phone off the hook just because he knew one of the bank managers. Think again. I have someone checking on me multiple times a day who appears to be an absolute gentleman.

SMS—Hi Lance, how have you been?

How long would it take Mr. Busy to respond this time? I had a few errands to run before meeting Khan for game night. I jumped in the shower and let the European shower head splash California's polluted water on my body. I grabbed the loafah sponge and squeezed the silky Dove body wash into it. I began exfoliating my skin and enjoying the feel of the loafah. I admired my body and how toned I kept it; I just wish someone of the opposite sex could appreciate the educated mind that went with it. The water continued splashing against my skin as I washed my face and rinsed it. When I got out of the shower and started to dry off, I felt the stubble on my legs and around heaven. I considered jumping back in the shower to Nair, but it didn't matter today. No one would see my legs and no one was definitely entering heaven today or in the morning regardless, of how well the evening went. My beautification dilemma was interrupted by my phone. I went to the table and saw it was a text from KINKO.

SMS—Hi Ms. Jordan, I really apologize. My current project is taking longer than expected. I would like to see you soon for lunch, dinner, or a drink.

My feet were getting cold standing there with the towel wrapped around me contemplating whether I should respond immediately. I put the phone back on the table and continued getting dressed. I turned the TV on for some company. Two tickets held winning numbers to America's legalized numbers game. News about the new coaching decision on an L.A. NBA teams was on. The sports analysts were going back and forth about the new coach and why the team didn't bring back some guy from Montana known as the Zen. One of the analysts that had the hairline and forehead like Sade got very animated as he spoke about the lack of respect shown by not bringing back the coach from Montana and that the new spotlight team of L.A. was the other team with a red-haired kid doing Hyundai

Empty Soul for Hire

commercials. I pulled out a matching midnight blue bra and panty set and put on a pair of Lucky jeans and a printed blouse. I threw on a pair of flats to give my feet a break. Then I got another text message.

SMS—Good morning Jordan! I'm looking forward to seeing you this evening.

Khan's application for the open position was looking better and better. I replied to Khan's message with a smiley face. I scrolled up to the earlier text message and typed my reply.

SMS reply—Hi Lance, no problem. I've been a little busy myself. The invite sounds good. Let's see if our schedules agree.

I got my keys and purse to head out and I heard my phone again. Okay Khan, I will see you later on, no need for us to text all day. But the message was from KINKO.

SMS—Sounds good Jordan, I should finish in a day or two. How about during the week?

Oh! Now he's got time for me. It all depends on how game night goes.

SMS reply—Hard to say. Let me know a day and I'll let you know.

SMS—I will do that.

Wow, two responses within minutes after *days* of no communication. Men can tell when a woman's moving on because the moment she turns her attention away, the man starts doing all he can to get that attention back. Well Mr. Kinkos you should have thought about that before you went days without responding or at least a phone call. At this rate, my ad will be closed and the position will be filled by a school teacher and first-time home buyer. My cell phone rang. The display screen again showed KINKO—OMG. I stared at the phone then picked it up. My cancer bound texting finger rubbed the green answer key, but didn't push it. My phone would ring three more times before going to voicemail. With my finger holding steady over the green key, I wanted to push it and sound happy to hear the voice on the other end. I really did.

Hi, this is Jordan sorry I missed your call please leave a message and I will return your call at my earliest convenience. Have a blessed day . . . beep

I locked the front door of my condo and headed into the brisk SoCal morning air. By the time I got to my car I heard my phone again. KINKO had left a voicemail. I sat in my assigned parking space and listened to Lance's message.

Hi Jordan, I was tired of texting so I decided to call. I'm sure our schedules can make room for a meet and greet. Like I said via text, this project is taking longer than I expected. I had every intention of getting with you sooner than this. I haven't been able to stop thinking about your smile. If you're not busy when I'm done, let's do our best to make it happen between us. Take care and feel free to call me back.

My automated cellular voice came on and gave instructions to either save the message or delete it. I saved the message this time, then pulled out of my parking space and headed to the gas station to fill up before driving to Khan's friend's house. I still didn't feel comfortable telling Khan where I lived. As I drove, I thought about Lance's voicemail. Was Lance worth it? What was he really about? And why did he need $60,000 in cash? Why not a cashier's check or an official check? That part never sat well with me. Khan was charming with a passion for his career but I had to admit I wasn't as attracted to him as I was to KINKO. Perhaps I need a reality check on what attractiveness is. Was it mental or physical? My brain didn't respond to the question. Instead my check engine light was glowing ever brighter as the days of no maintenance grew. Hell men got them a little piece and kept it moving with no emotions all the time; why couldn't I? I couldn't because I was a fervid person that had to connect with a man before I let them into heaven. After I let them in, though, everything went to hell faster than new reality shows came on TV. Maybe I should just get the check engine light taken care of and keep praying for the man God wants me to have and not hire a regular service mechanic LOL.

I stopped by the utility companies and paid my monthly bills. I was still old-school in that regard and didn't pay my bills online. Working at the bank had taught me well about online identity theft and the headaches customers went through proving their innocence. I stopped by my favorite Jamaican spot off Crenshaw and picked up some jerk chicken with rice and beans. I didn't eat everybody's cooking and I didn't know what finger food meant at Khan's friend's house. While I waited for my order, I caught a young kid with dreads looking at my booty. I didn't entertain his immature flirting. When the heavy accented Jamaican lady called my number I put a little extra something in my walk. Even in the flat shoes my booty still was tight and my hips swayed like the black Cali sensation who was the first sister to grace the cover of Sports Illustrated swimsuit edition. I left the kid's young eyes with something to think about. When I got home, I ate the Caribbean chicken and looked through my mail; nothing but junk mail and bills. I had enough time to get a nap in, so I flossed and brushed my teeth before lying down. I cracked my window and felt the Santa Ana winds waft through my bedroom. The winds battled the smog on a daily basis. You'd be lucky to see downtown on a good day. The alarm on my cell phone woke me up at 4:15 PM. I got up and looked in my closet to see what I was going to wear to game night. Khan said it was casual so a nice pair of jeans and top with a low heel should be enough. I picked out a pair of 7 for all mankind jeans and DKNY top. I sent Khan a text to get the address. He didn't respond quickly like he normally does so I jumped in the shower. The whispering sound of my check engine light was humming in my ears while I showered. I ignored its agonizing criticism. *Girl I'm running on empty over here, my oil levels are low, my tires need to be balanced and rotated. Come on Jordan just get me a little maintenance, don't you want me to run for another 100,000 miles? Come on . . . . please just a little maintenance . . . Khan seems to be a certified mechanic . . .* So I shaved my legs and heaven as the voice of carnal knowledge faded into the bathroom fan. I dried off and turned on my flat iron to do something with my mane. Black or pink undies? I don't know where the panties are to match the pink bra. Black it is. I heard my cell phone, it was Khan. I wrote down the address and told him I would be there at 7 sharp. I finished getting dressed and headed out. L.A. traffic was super heavy on the weekends thanks to the highway maintenance department folks who had decided to extend freeways on the weekend.

My GPS told me I had twelve minutes to my destination. I sent Khan a text and told him I was eleven minutes. He said he'd be outside waiting. I turned down the residential street and was immediately impressed by the city of Carson's classy landscape. I couldn't say that for other L.A. County neighborhoods that had been overrun by drugs, drug dealers, and people who didn't value home ownership. Many neighborhoods were infested with renters and didn't have many original homeowners left. As I got close to the address in my GPS I could see Khan standing on the sidewalk. That voice from the shower got in the passenger seat: *mmm mmm look at 'em girl, he's a well-dress mechanic and a gentleman . . . . go ahead, and pull into his bay and get you some maintenance.*

I let the passenger window down and Khan came up to the car,

"Hi Jordan, how are you?"

"I'm well, Where should I park?"

"Mind if I get in and we can find something?" a *gentleman, girl*

I unlocked the door and he hopped in. When he got in I thought he leaned close like he wanted a kiss. I didn't lean in, I applied my foot to the gas pedal to find a parking spot.

"Something should be up here."

"Is a lot of people in there?"

Empty Soul for Hire

"It's a few, why?"

"Well this is only our second date, don't want to feel uncomfortable."

"If you start to feel that way we can leave."

"Okay, or you can stay, they're your friends."

"Jordan, you're funny. There's a spot. Can you parallel park?"

I smiled and put my car in reverse paying no attention to the DMV employee in the passenger seat. When I got to the sidewalk Khan had his hand out. Was he serious? Okay I'll hold his hand but I hope he doesn't think this will continue inside. I won't be rude in front of a bunch of folks I don't know, but Mr. Banana Republic better get it together.

The house was nicely decorated and everyone spoke when we walked in. Khan played it just right. He didn't introduce me with a personal title, just a simple introduction. Music was playing and a huge flat screen TV was on showing the Trojans game. There was lots of food and drinks. The guys were watching the game and lying to one another; the ladies were gathered in the kitchen gossiping. Khan stayed close and didn't leave me alone. One of the ladies in the kitchen came in the living room and grabbed the TV remote and turned the TV out. The guys in the living room gave her a bewildered look but remained silent. She told all the guys to stand up and go get their dates, wives, girlfriends, or flavor of the weekend. Everyone was paired up and the first game began.

The game was called Sip or Sit Quietly. Each person was given two index cards and on the cards you had to write two things you've done sexually but phrase it like you never did. The cards were shuffled and the questions began. If you had done what the index card said then you took a sip of your drink, or else sat quietly. At first I wasn't sure if I would be honest when an index card came up that applied to me. After all I didn't want Khan to know all the things I'd done sexually. What the hell, it's all in fun.

I've never had sex with other people in the room

I observed the people lifting their cups to sip. Khan hadn't lifted his cup but I knew the truthful answer; I took a sip.

Have you ever received oral sex while driving

I knew I had given while the other person was driving but hadn't been on the receiving end. Just about all of the men lifted their cups, including Khan. I was blown away when I saw two of the women lift their cups. Even one of the men looked and asked if they were on the *receiving* end. Both women nodded their heads—Yes. Everybody laughed out loud. The other women gave them high fives. After a while the confessions on the cards became ordinary ones that just about everyone over 25 had done. The catch was, if everyone felt comfortable with their date to admit it. This game continued until all the index cards were read. The games continued with Dirty Minds and Taboo. The atmosphere was nice. I didn't feel any pressure and Khan didn't give me dirty looks for the confessions I drank to or for how I answered the questions of the other games.

It was close to 11:00 PM and a few couples had left. Some of the guys had started slamming the white ivory with black dots and instigating with the other players. I sat with the women watching reruns of "Basketball Wives of L.A." I checked my phone and saw I had two text messages. One from Miriam and the other was from KINKO. Khan was standing looking at the fellas slam bones as they yelled out *Dime, Fifteen cents*. When he looked over at me I whispered "It's getting late." He smiled and walked over to me,

"Are you ready to go?"

"Yeah, it's getting late and you know how the freeway gets this time of night."

"No problem. Let me say my goodbyes and we can roll."

"Oh no, you can stay. I just would like you to walk me to my car."

"No, I'm leaving when you leave babe."

Did he just call me babe?

"Are you sure?"

"Yes, I'll be right back."

I hope Khan wasn't leaving and hoping he was coming back to my place. This date was over. I had a good time and his friends were nice but I need a follow-up interview before I let him into heaven. When he came back he was grinning like a little kid at the San Diego Zoo feeding the monkeys,

"What's so funny?" I asked.

"Nothing, I'm just glad you enjoyed yourself."

"How do you know I enjoyed myself?"

"If a lady doesn't like the scene, she politely leaves soon after arriving."

"Tushay."

"Give a brother some credit."

"Okay, Okay you right."

"So do you have to get right home?"

"I would like to head home. What's up?"

"The night's young and I'm really enjoying you; just not ready for it to end."

"What did you have in mind?"

"Feel like going to the Seabird Lounge down in Long Beach, we could catch the last set?"

I thought about his invite and knew the later the night got the more tired I'd be and wouldn't feel like driving home. I wasn't trying to spend the night at his place but I was feeling the vibe of his company. *Go head girl go, go, go and listen to some music. Get me some maintenance please.* The voice of deprived carnal knowledge was back.

"Okay, are we taking two cars or one?"

"Your car is safe here."

I followed Khan down Avalon to the 405 freeway. I heard the Seabird Lounge was nice but I hadn't been to it. Sometimes the DJ's on 94.7 the wave would talk about a headliner playing there as well as the local talent and the premier drink specials. The city of Long Beach had been rebuilt and its night life was gaining attention around SoCal. As we got closer to downtown Long Beach, I could see the lights of the Queen Mary and the beautiful tall streetlights of the downtown avenues. When we turned on Ocean Avenue, I was amazed to see that the once dead city was born again, with new restaurants and little pub spots. The lounge had a line around the building. I was already prepared to tell Khan I would just get back on the freeway and head home: I wasn't standing in line at this hour to get into a club. Khan turned his signal on to enter one of the parking garages; I flashed my high beams twice. He came to a stop and came back to my car,

"Hey that was a long line and I really don't feel like standing outside." I said discouragingly.

"Me either; I know the bouncers at the door."

"Are you sure Khan?"

"Yes Jordan."

"Okay."

He went back to his car and we pulled into the parking garage. After we parked and started to walk towards the lounge Khan leaned in and whispered "thank you" in my ear. Great, just what that the little voice in my body wanted to hear. I politely responded with "you're welcome." Khan wasn't lying; we walked right past the line to the front. He and the bouncer gave each other the brotherly love fist over fist pound and then touched knuckles and just like that we were inside. I need that kind of hook-up all the time when I go out. Inside there was a saxophonist blasting an old tune by Stevie Wonder. The people sitting at their tables were grooving to the tunes. Khan must have called while we were on the freeway because we had a table reserved. I was impressed. He pulled my chair out too, nothing like the commoners of L.A. Khan ordered a rum and diet coke with a lime. I ordered Hennessey on the rocks. Khan smiled after the waitress left. It was kind of hard to talk over the live music, but Khan tried to hold small talk,

"So what did you think of my friends?"

"They seem like good people."

"I think so, I met most of them a couple of years ago at education workshop."

"Oh okay, that's cool."

"So Ms. Jordan, do you think I can see you again?"

I smiled but didn't answer immediately. I played like the music was too loud and asked him what did he say? He repeated his question immediately.

"Yes that's possible, but let's take things slow."

"At your pace it is, my friend."

He leaned back in his chair and faced the stage. I wasn't sure if he was upset or just respecting my answer and not pushing it. When the waitress returned with our drinks, Khan held his drink up. Oh my, what are we toasting to?

"To the pacesetter!" he said arrogantly.

In a way I didn't like his arrogance but at the same time I was a little turned on. I raised my glass and looked at him as intimately as I could and said: "To me!"

Khan smiled a sinister smile back at me like he was the officiator of a track meet who had just squeezed the trigger of the starting gun for the race to begin.

Twenty

I **sat in front** of the depleted attorney. His head was slumped down and he smelled ripe. His right foot was crushed and turning colors. I slapped him to get his attention. When he looked up his face was no longer looking rich and smooth. The after-five shadow didn't fit his Ivy-League appeal and his hair needed more of whatever expensive hair product he used. I told him to open his mouth. He didn't so immediately. I shook the bottle of water in one hand and the mouthwash in the other. It was his choice, but I was only going to ask him one more time. I motioned the bottle of water towards him and he opened his mouth, I poured a little water in. Clearly he didn't appreciate my gesture. He spit the water in my face and shook his head. I punched him in his empty gut and he coughed.

"You're really making this harder than it has to be." I said.

"I told you I don't know . . ."

I didn't let him finish his lying sentence. I punched him again and covered his head with a black hood. I went to the water hose and filled a bucket. When I came back to his malodorous presence I held my breath, then got in his face and said,

"Mr. Bach, is this going to be a short day or a long day?"

Empty Soul for Hire

"That depends on you, you heartless bastard." His voice was muffled behind the hood.

"I don't have the answers I need so it really depends on you sir."

"Save your feeble kindness."

"Have it your way."

I lifted the bucket, ready to begin the ancient torture known as waterboarding when I heard a buzzing noise. I felt my pocket; it wasn't my cell phone. It was Phil's cell phone buzzing in his pants pocket. The attorney turned his head in my direction. I was sure he was grinning behind the hood. I pulled the annoying sound from his pocket. The screen showed blocked number. I didn't answer the phone. I assumed whoever was calling had the latest cell phone tracker ready to begin tracing our location. The attorney inside the hood said: "You know what that buzzing means?"

"It doesn't mean anything unless I press a button to connect the call."

"You will, because you want answers."

"I won't because I don't know who's calling your undeserving ass."

"I'm very deserving. You're the one that's going to wish you'd never come to Ballys."

I laughed and pushed his chair over towards the wall and propped it against the wall. I lifted the bucket of water and began pouring it over his hooded face. I heard him struggling as he tried to catch his breath and shake away the water. I gave him a break like the Navy Seals take when they train in 40-foot pools. I heard him gasping for every worthless breath of air he had left. I walked over to my duffle bag and pulled out my cell phone tracking scrambler. I connected it to the attorney's cell phone for the next call. The party calling was possibly a piece to this puzzle and they were getting worried. It wasn't his wife calling; I'm sure his affluent colleagues had called her and told her a believable lie about her dear Phil. I refilled the bucket and went back over to Phil. He was breathing heavy and had the chills. His Egyptian cotton shirt was drenched and no longer wrinkle-free,

"The witnesses, Phil!"

No response. I could hear him breathing, but he was a stubborn cuss.

"The witnesses, Phil!" I repeated.

"And just like that you're going to let me go free?" He asked.

"I told you what I wanted. Lawyers like you are a dime a dozen. You've gotten rich representing Banderas and lying about his case. I'm sure he can find another scum attorney willing and able to represent him."

My political speech was interrupted by another buzz. I took the wet hood off of Phil's head and made sure my tracking scrambler was in place before connecting with the unknown caller. I pressed the green talk button but didn't say anything. The unknown caller heard me breathing. I heard him making sure his cell phone tracker was working. My scrambler was direct from the supply room of the agency located in Langley, Virginia. I remained quiet and heard the connection getting distorted. Our devices were battling with each other, mine having the upper hand at the moment. A voice finally broke through: "Is Phil alive?"

"Who is this?"

"Is Phil Alive?" the voice repeated.

"We can play this game a few more ticks then I'm disconnecting."

"We need to talk."

"My mother told me not to talk to strangers."

"Is your mother there holding your murderous hand? You left the kiddie playground a long time ago."

"Tell me who you are or you'll hear about Phil on the news and you can take your decoder back for a refund."

The phone was silent for a few seconds. I had already slid my thumb over to the red button ready to disconnect. The unknown caller offered an alias: "Call me Eduardo."

"What do you want, Eduardo?"

"I need to know if Phil is alive or dead?"

"Why? Are you part of the rescue team?"

He laughed

"Listen to me, Phil is of no consequence. We rented him just like you're being rented by your high-paying coward clients. He can be replaced with a snap of a finger and I'm sure you're not indispensable. So is Phil alive or dead?"

"He's alive for now. He has some questions to answer."

"The questions you have don't matter because Banderas' fate lies with witnesses who won't see another sunset."

Eduardo hung up, the trace no longer mattered to him. He had made his point clear to me and I needed to pass that message on to my associates. The ingrate attorney sat there wondering what my ears heard on the other end of his cell phone. I left him there to

Empty Soul for Hire

his own thoughts. I needed to make a phone call. When I stepped outside two envelopes appeared on my display screen; in the midst of my erotic conversation with Eduardo I didn't feel my phone buzz. Voicemails would have to wait.

SMS—We need to talk immediately.

I expected a quick response but it didn't come. This wasn't like my associates. My mind raced as fast as the Jamaican sprinter that broke Olympic records. I had been thrown in the middle of a war so many young Americans were fighting and dying for in Afghanistan? A meaningless and costly war for the poppy seed and opium trade except this war was right in America's backyard, a war over a cash crop for cannabis sativa—*marijuana*. It seems like the more states try to legalize it for medicinal purposes, the higher the number of murders and turf wars were occurring. In the '60s the hippies smoked marijuana in their carefree world minus the violence, then in the '70s cannabis became a drug bringing in small profits on local street corners in black neighborhoods, occasionally reaching the suburbs. But there was respect. People knew who had the good herb and who had the weak, but they didn't kill each other. The less potent dealer would take his product to an unexposed area and set up shop. As the economy changed along with the overall mentality of America, the killings slowly started to rise. Our society has become a civilization of greed and no regard for hard work and sacrifice. The mentality "is somebody has it and I don't, so I will do what it takes to get it *by any means necessary,*"; the phrase coined from the French play Dirty Hands. The phrase entered into the popular culture when the late Malcolm X used it in one of his last speeches. My cell phone buzzed. It was a text reply from my associates.

SMS reply—Do you know the location of the witnesses?

SMS—No.

My cell phone buzzed; now I had the attention of my associates. I answered with a slight attitude, "Yep!"

"Is he still holding on to the location of the witnesses?"

"Yes, and to be honest I don't think the location is important."

"What do you mean?"

"I should let you know that Phil met with some people in California before he came back to Tampa. I believe those people know where the witnesses are and plan to kill them?"

"What people in California?"

"Does the name Eduardo mean anything to you?"

"Not that I recall."

"He called on the attorney's cell phone and wanted to know if Bach was still alive. He also said Banderas' fate was sealed and the witnesses wouldn't see another sunset."

"When was this conversation?"

"Just before I sent you the text message."

"And he didn't say anything else?"

My phone beeped. I had another call coming in. I looked at the phone; it was Jordan. This girl's timing was impeccable.

"No he didn't. He hung up after that."

"Were you able to trace the call?"

"No I was worried about them tracing the call so I had the scrambler connected."

Silence on the other end.

Empty Soul for Hire

"He's bluffing, beat the shit out of him and find those witnesses."

"What about Eduardo?"

"He didn't give you a last name?"

"No he didn't."

"I will put the name out there and see what comes back."

"What if Eduardo calls again?"

"Hopefully I will have some intel for you when we speak again."

"Okay."

"I'm surprised it's taken you this long to get the information."

"Noted."

"We'll be in touch."

The caller disconnected before I could respond. I had more questions now and I was going to get answers one way or another. Before I walked back in the house I pulled a heavy duty portable battery charger from the trunk of the Challenger. I didn't say a word to the inglorious person sharing space with me. I walked past him to the back of the house into the garage and began tearing the ceiling out. The drywall steadily fell to the ground until the open ceiling was exposed. I saw several wood beams above me but I needed one the right height to hang his emaciated body from. I slung a rope over one of the beams and missed. The rope landed next to me and laughed at me. I tried again, barely catching the beam; I pulled the rope to even the braids of yarn and tied a knot in the slaughterhouse hook. When I returned the repulsive area smelled like urine, days of old funk, and gas. I stood Phil up. His body felt frail and his polished look had diminished. He looked like he had been in a Turkish prison.

"The witnesses!"

He didn't say anything.

"Who did you meet with in San Pedro? Was it Eduardo?"

No words. Just as I was about to ask another question, Phil's inside gave in and I saw him getting ready to vomit. I pushed him back in the chair and he leaned forward. He regurgitated the last meal he ate right in front of me. I felt no compassion; I didn't offer him a cold towel or anything to settle his stomach. I just stood there. After he puked again, I came closer to him and tied his wrist with rope and cut the zip ties. He looked surprised as if he thought I would be stupid and cut the zip ties first. I'm not a rookie to situations like these. I stood him up again and walked what was left of his body to the garage. Call me patient but I asked again: "The witnesses? Did you meet with Eduardo in San Pedro?"

His swollen eyes looked at me and his swollen red lips mustered the strength to crack a smile. I stepped back and gave him a round kick to his right jaw. He fell back on the floor of the garage. He was a stubborn bastard. He laid there looking at me intensely. I returned the intense look. My stare was broken when I felt the buzz in my pocket. It was his phone again—another unknown caller. I ran and got the scrambler before pressing the green talk button and said:

"Let me guess. Eduardo?"

The voice on the other end laughed

"Where's Phil?"

"He's lying on the ground smelling like piss with swollen eyes and a bloodied lip."

"So you're torturing him?"

"No, we're playing Twister."

"A comedian?"

"I'm busy. Unless you have something important to say I have to get back to the Twister game. It's my turn to spin."

"Has Phil answered your questions? Not that the answers will help you or the people that hired you. Banderas and the Colombians are finished, witnesses or not."

"Is that right?"

"Senor, a lot of blood has been spilled and it will continue until the Solderota Cartel has full reign. We need information from the attorney as well."

"Oh now you need him?"

"It's a business decision. I could care less for the disgusting pig."

"Mutually agreed. Enough of the small talk."

"Si si, so are you going to kill him?"

"Are you getting sentimental now? Thought you didn't care about the disgusting pig?"

"He is indeed a pig, but I do need him Senor."

"And I need the location of the witnesses."

"Stop asking about the witnesses hombre."

"Well we don't have anything else to discuss."

No response immediately. Then he asked,

"How much are they paying you to torture the attorney for the witnesses?"

"That doesn't matter, but if you must know, I'm not working for minimum wage."

"You're funny amigo."

"Now we're friends?"

"Far from friends. I want to rip your throat out."

"Give it your best shot. Many have tried."

"You're really a cockroach amongst black widow spiders. Are you sure you want to continue this testosterone foreplay?"

"You called me, remember?"

"Bottom line is we knew the attorney would keep eating from both plates. Instead of choosing, his greed got the best of him. Now we intend to do some eating of our own. Let that hideous mulatto know I have his wife and his beautiful daughters. His wife is tied to a bed with her legs spread open and my young soldiers are enjoying her as we speak. And his daughters won't be able to wear white dresses at the altar if you don't stop jerking me around *pendejo*."

I didn't respond to the grotesque situation my ears heard. I held the phone and looked at Phil lying there like a lamb waiting to be slaughtered. This was my chance to see what Phil was really made of. Was he really that selfish, or did he have any feelings left for his children. His wife would never be the same after the repeated forcible violations. But, she made her choice how she wanted to live. His daughters still had a choice, but their fate lay in his pitiful existence. I went for it and said: "Eduardo has your family Phil!"

His body wiggled and he looked up at me; his eyes so wide you would have thought he had a thyroid condition.

"You're joking. Eduardo knows what I'm capable of."

I was hoping the bilingual goon on the other end could hear the conversation clearly. I showed the cell phone to Phil for him to see the call in progress. I didn't care. Something had to give with the missing puzzle pieces. I continued the verbal attack . . .

"His soldiers have already raped your wife repeatedly and your daughters are next!"

Again I spoke loud enough for the other party to hear the conversation. The attorney dropped his head in despair. There was a brief silence throughout the garage. Then I heard the sound of sulking and sniffles come from the ground. Did the mention of his daughters or his wife being repeatedly invaded give him a spiritual strength to do the right thing for once in his life? Or would he go out in a blaze with no regard for the collateral damage his actions caused?

"Okay, tell that bean eating wetback I said he'll never take over."

I had struck a fire under the egotistical attorney and I cracked a smile. I knew the stakes had gone up higher than the odds of the Mayweather and Pacquiao fight,

"Eduardo, did you hear that?"

"Si Senor, I did."

Before I could respond, Eduardo hung up the phone. Phil was lying on the ground crying. I pulled out my cell and sent a text message.

SMS—Call me ASAP. It's Urgent.

Phil was born again, his voice was clear and not cracking. He asked me politely to untie his legs and sit him up. He had stop crying and his face was fire engine red. I could see the hatred in his eyes. I welcomed his new look. Although my tree of life had no branches, I knew the sacrifices I would make for my children and I hoped Phil felt the same for his branches. I untied him and set him up. He said: "We don't have a lot of time. You need to listen very carefully."

"I'm listening."

Why hadn't my associate called me back? I will make sure to mention that like he mentioned me taking so long,

"I need to get to my yacht in Clearwater."

"Why?"

"To give you what Eduardo's looking for. Don't let your arrogance get my daughters raped or worse."

"Calm down with the new found conscience. You should have thought of all this before you got in bed with these thoughtless people."

"And you're a saint, right?"

I disliked the person before my eyes, but his comment hurt. It made me think of my future and whethe I would ever grow any branches on my tree. How much pain and suffering would they have to endure because of my past? Would the families of those I killed come after my seed in retaliation? My public profile was nonexistent thanks to the people I knew. I'm learning now that everyone has a price and that the person willing to pay the most will get whatever they want. I was no exception. I was merely in good standing because of my skill and kill rate. I would get old and not be as quick or skilled someday. Then like a pair of Evander Holyfield's boxing gloves on Ebay for sale, my personal information would be for sale as well. Phil yelled something at me and broke me out of my daze. I snapped and yelled.

"What?"

"We have to get out of here."

"Calm down; they don't know where we are."

"Are you sure?"

"You're an attorney, right?"

"What's your point?"

"Let me handle this. Tell me what or who's at your yacht."

"Get me to my yacht safely and you'll have all you need. Trust me."

"You weren't so giving before. Why now?"

"Are you going to stand here and have dialogue with me or are we going to Clearwater?"

"We'll get there; just sit there and enjoy the few minutes of being the new good person you've become."

"I am a good person."

"If your own vote counts then you are."

Our gracious dialogue was interrupted when my phone buzzed. I answered with attitude again: "Yep."

"What's so urgent?"

"Do you have any intel on Eduardo?"

"Not yet."

"Well I do. He's with the Solderota Cartel. They have Phil's family and he still won't say where the witnesses are, which is really not an issue at this point. His clan is prepared to dismantle Banderas' organization. Phil claims there's something or someone at his yacht that will give us everything we need. Do you know what he's talking about?"

"Let me talk to him."

"He's tied up at the moment, I'll put the phone on speaker."

"Okay."

"Go ahead; you're on speaker."

"See what greed gets you Phil?" my associate asked.

Silence from Phil. My associate was irritated beyond belief

"Answer me you prick."

Phil was just looking at me, not saying a word.

"I don't think he's going to answer you." I told my associate.

"Fair enough. I know what's at his yacht. Take the stubborn prick there and text me when you get there. Spare no lives if you have to when you get to the yacht."

"Okay."

Twenty One

I was surprised I stayed at the Seabird lounge until the last set finished. The music was flowing and Khan and I even danced to a couple of the songs. The bartender was making the drinks just right and I got a slight buzz, not to the point I couldn't drive though. As we were leaving, I could see a few females checking Khan out and looking me up and down. Women were notorious for checking out a man when he was with another woman and looking the woman up and down. That's how the disrespect starts. Next they're discreetly sliding their number to him. I grabbed Khan's hand as we walked out. I felt him jerk a little but he didn't look at me; he played it cool. It was a little nippy outside. The rose man was at the door with the one-rose and three-rose bouquets. I always thought that was funny. Most men could barely remember birthdays, anniversaries, or the day of love but would drop $5 or $10 heading out the door of a club to get some points, hoping they were getting in the sheets later. If men only knew; a woman most times knows when she's going to have sex long before a man *thinks* he's going to get sex from her. I was happy when Khan politely declined the solicitor. When we got outside, Khan lifted our hands in the air and asked: "What's this about?"

I gave him an evasive smile.

"Nothing, I just felt like holding your hand that's all."

"The pacesetter." He said in a laughing voice.

We both laughed as we walked to the parking garage. When we got to our cars, that awkward moment was right there standing between us. Do we kiss? Do we hug? Or just say we had a nice time and say our goodnights? Khan was standing directly in front of me looking in my eyes. I could tell he was doing the mental countdown before trying to kiss me. I beat him to zero and came to his lips for a quick kiss then told him I had a really nice time. In fact better than I thought it would be.

"I'm glad you had a good time."

"I am too."

"Just curious, what kind of pace are you going to set?" he asked.

"You're funny."

"No seriously, I just would like to know so I don't make you feel smothered or myself look desperate."

"So you're *not* desperate?"

"No I like you and all but . . ."

"But what?"

"I'm not trying to play myself if you're just *dating* and not looking for a relationship."

Am I drunk or did this man mention the word relationship in a conversation? Are you kidding me? I should hire him right now and seal the new hire process with some loving and a cooked meal in the morning. Slow down Jordan. He's a nice conversation piece like all the others then shortly after the loving and a few meals, he'll need his space and want to hang with his boys.

"Khan I'm not just dating but I'm not rushing into anything either. I'm only talking to you at the moment."

I gave his ego a little boost but didn't kick it into overdrive and have him thinking we're exclusive. After all, I did call Lance while we were driving to the Seabird Lounge. What is it about KINKO that I can't shake?

"Okay cool. I can respect that. Are you okay driving home?" he asked

"Yes I can make it."

"If you don't mind would you call or text me and let me know you made it home?"

"Sure."

He opened my car door for me and didn't force the issue with another kiss. He said good night and walked to his car. I hopped back on the 605 freeway praying the 405 freeway wasn't a parking lot. I turned the radio on to KJLH and listened to the oldies as I headed home. I have to admit a small piece of me wanted to give Khan some loving tonight but I just couldn't bring myself to do it. If he's genuine then we'll get to that in due time and it won't feel awkward or rushed. The radio station was playing Al *"hot grits"* Green's "Love and Happiness." I turned my radio up and started singing along with Al. This was music—"love will make you do right, love will make you do wrong, love will make you stay out all night long." My American Idol audition was rudely interrupted when I saw nothing but red brake lights ahead as I merged onto the 405—*Aggh!*

After creeping along at 45 mph, almost an hour later I was home. I called Khan and told him I made it home.

"Traffic must have been pretty bad?" he asked.

"Ridiculous!"

"Well I'm glad you're home, I'm sure you're tired."

"Thanks. I'll call you tomorrow."

"Okay good night Jordan."

"Good night."

I didn't want to get in bed with the club odor on me so I took a shower when I got off the phone. When I finished I turned on the TV before falling asleep. Late night gimmicks were on all the local channels. I didn't want to hear how to lose weight using some crappy fitness equipment or how I could get rich in real estate if I called in ninety seconds for the special low price. I turned to VH-1 soul player and Lauren Hill was singing *"Doo Wap."* I don't remember when I fell asleep but I didn't set the sleep timer and woke up to Run DMC screaming *"My Addidas."*

Twenty Two

I didn't have any plans for Sunday other than relaxing. Sundays are reserved for the Lifetime channel. They normally ran great movie marathons that have you smiling, crying, and in the end believing old-fashion love still exists. I opened my front door to get the Sunday *L.A. Times*. I hope Target had a sales paper this week and the Living section had some good articles. I scrambled some eggs and made some bacon before reading the paper. Sitting at the table, I read the front page headlines. More talk about the upcoming elections and how close the candidates were in the race. The critics talked about each candidate's views and what they had to do in order to win. The purple and gold basketball team of Los Angeles was still struggling in the win column under their new UnZen-like coach. Of course, the team's voice of Kobe Bryant was all over the article about his disappointment and idle threats of being traded. Meanwhile the unpopular basketball team of Los Angeles was gaining a stronger fan base and the win column for them was better than the thought-to-be championship team of L.A. I flipped to the World News section and got depressed reading about so much turmoil happening: Earthquakes in Guatemala, women activists slain in Afghanistan, more violence in the Mexico drug trade. The last article I read had a picture of a handsome guy smiling. He was a high-profile attorney for a Colombian drug lord that had gone missing. The small caption talked about how he had been filing unsuccessful appeals for one of the most notorious drug lords since

Escobar. New Edition's *"Mr. Telephone Man"* ringtone intruded the Sunday morning silence. I answered.

"Good morning Khan."

"How did you sleep?" he asked.

"Great! What about you?"

"Good. Hope I didn't disturb you."

"No I was reading the Sunday paper and about to have some breakfast. What's up?"

"I just came back from my morning jog; my pace was a 6-minute mile. I thought about you."

That was so corny.

"Oh is that right?"

"I know the line was cheesy."

"At least you're honest."

"Seriously Jordan I wanted to ask if you would join me this afternoon for a movie?"

"No football with the fellas?"

"Man, did I have on a caveman suit holding a stick last night?"

"Meaning?"

"I'm not in front of the TV for every sporting event."

"Calm down man. Growing up, my dad's Sunday was church, the Sunday paper, and football until it was dinner time. I thought it was a guy thing. My bad."

"Yeah okay! Is that a no on the movie?"

I sensed an attitude. I looked at my SHOES calendar on the wall and a nice pair of Giuseppe Zanotti was the feature shoe of the month. And I didn't see red marker for this week. My period wasn't coming, maybe his was. I swear men are more emotional than women.

"What movie did you have in mind?"

"It's a few good ones out. Did you have a preference?"

"*Skyfall.*"

"Wow! You like James Bond?"

"Did I have on a floral dress and a little dog in my arms looking for the *Wizard of Oz* last night?"

"Tushay."

"So are you good with *Skyfall*?"

"Let me check the show times. Any particular theater?"

"No I trust you."

"Do you?"

"To pick a movie location fool. Maybe you should jog a little slower next time."

"LOL! It's showing at Arc Light Beach Cities in El Segundo at 4:15."

"Where in the heck is that?"

"It's the theater by LAX next to PF Changs and across from McCormick & Schmick."

"Oh Okay. I've been there just never knew that was the name of it."

"So I'll see you there around 4?"

"Why didn't you offer to come pick me up?"

"Didn't think you felt comfortable with me knowing where you live?"

"You might be keeper. See you at 4."

"I see you like to play, Jordan . . . . Bye."

"Bye."

When I hung up with Khan I checked the Lifetime channel listing. I wanted to at least get one movie in before going to the movies. I called Miriam. I knew she was dying to hear how the night went.

Twenty Three

Phil was sitting with a look of serious regard. He had to be wondering what my associate had told me to do with him. After I took the phone off of speaker all he heard was me say okay. I sent a text message to my Tampa contact and told them I needed a new mode of transportation. The Challenger still had plenty muscle under the hood but the damage from playing bumper cars on the expressway would definitely get attention. I'm sure the Tampa Police Department was looking for me and my born again prisoner. I had to wrap the situation up quickly. I couldn't deal with any commotion en route to the hidden prize at Phil's yacht. My contact responded and said they'd be here in thirty minutes or less. I wasn't the leader of an organized crime group but as a one-man clipper I had some of the loyalist contacts in the free world. They responded efficiently and quickly; former military men and women that no longer trusted the U.S. Government and were off the public grid in every traceable facet. Phil's impatience interrupted my thoughts: "Are you going to untie me now?"

"Why should I do that?"

"We are acquainted now wouldn't you say?"

"No I wouldn't say. You started crying like a bundle of joy in a hospital nursery. Now we're acquainted; so much for being a new person."

"Your arrogance escapes me."

"Listen, Phil, because of your decisions and greed you've destroyed a lot of lives including your wife's. Instead of keeping your practice honest you jumped at the opportunity of stardom to represent a famous thug, then jumped in bed with the competition and started playing both sides. Now you hear your wife has been ravished by a bunch of immature wetback dicks and your daughters might be next, you want to repent and all's going to be forgiven? The unmitigated gall"

"And I guess you don't have children or someone you love?"

"That's none of your business."

"You're callous."

"Don't judge until you've been judged."

"Are you going to let me freshen up?"

"This isn't the movies Phil; where the prisoner is well treated with nice meals and hotel honors rewards service. I'm stuck with your robust scent until further notice, care for some almonds?"

"Bastard!"

"Such kind words from the new disciple."

I heard two cars pull up outside. I went to the window. A set of headlights flashed twice at the house. I stood Phil up and put a fresh hood over his face and a fresh set of zip ties over his wrist. I heard him sigh. I ignored to his juvenile smirks. I grabbed my duffle bag and looked around one last time before leaving the abandoned house.

"Hey guys."

"How's it going? Damn he smells bad, man. Why don't you clean him up?"

"You sound like him with the special requests." He handed me a set of keys.

"Here you go. Tanks full and registration's legit. We'll take care of the Challenger."

I knew Phil's ear perked up when he heard the chatter, listening for clues or hints. He still had hope.

"Thanks. I'll be in touch."

I put the polluted passenger in the Crown Victoria. I didn't remove his hood immediately but buckled his seat belt.

"This is absurd." He said.

"Please shut up with the comments."

"Really. What can I do at this point if you untie me?"

"We won't find out. Now shut up."

I closed his door and bid farewell to my contacts. They pulled off but left the Challenger. I guess they were coming back later to get it. I started the Crown Victoria—nothing like the sound of the Challenger but it would do for now. I put my new getaway car in drive. Before I got 20 feet Phil was at it again:

"I can't tell you where my yacht is with this hood on."

"Your Mangusta yacht is at the Clearwater Harbor Marina Club. I just need the slip number and you don't need the hood off to tell me that, do you?"

"Who *are* you?"

I didn't answer and kept driving. Shortly after we got on the dirt road I heard a loud explosion and saw the bright colors of yellow and burnt orange ascend into the air. I saw the American muscle machine receive a religious send off in my rearview mirror. Before we turned onto the major highway I took off Phil's hood and gave him specific instructions:

"If you lift your arms to show any passing cars you're zip-tied, that will be the last thing you remember before I kill you."

For the first time since we became *acquainted* he looked like he actually thought he might die. His silent acknowledgment was all I needed.

Driving over the Courtney Campbell Causeway my mind drifted to Jordan and how I would explain my sporadic communications with her. I wasn't going to seem desperate for her time and understanding but at least wanted to apologize and let her know I was interested in getting to know her. The timing and stubbornness of my passenger was really agitating me. I hadn't checked on Catalina or the store. Catalina wasn't too much of a concern. She could tell if I'd been home or not so she wouldn't cook anything. She'd kick back in the family room and watch Telemundo until 3:00 PM then she'd watch the lady from the "Today" show who had her own show now. If she hadn't heard from me by 2:00 PM she wouldn't cook and just leave at 4:30. I trusted Catalina. I'm sure the employees at the store didn't miss me one bit and were probably giving their friends discounts on supplies and taking long breaks. I wonder if Jordan was dating anyone or if I was rebound thing? Perhaps I should leave her alone altogether since she works at one of the banks where I do business. If the relationship didn't work out between us, things could turn ugly. I was impressed she remembered me from the Conga Room, that's rare in Los Angeles. She has me curious.

Exiting the causeway into Clearwater the streets were empty with a couple of cars moving about. Phil's cell phone rang. The screen showed unknown caller; Eduardo I presume. I didn't answer. After the ringing stopped, the phone began ringing again with the

Empty Soul for Hire

same display name. I ignored it again. Until I got to the attorney's yacht and secured the missing piece of this territorial war game I had no time for Eduardo's trivial dialogue. By now he either had the witnesses or had killed them. Finding their location was insignificant at this point. Listening to the description of his bestial soldiers having their way with Phil's wife wasn't entertaining to me. The inestimable possession aboard the sea vessel was the only thing that could possibly save his daughters and satisfy my associates. The girl's mother would need capacious therapy to regain her sense of womanhood and self-respect. The self-help section at the local bookstore or community group talks wouldn't be enough for her. She needed heavily medicated assistance to get over her recent encounters enough to be a benevolent mother to her daughters.

The smell of the bay disturbed my passenger as he wrestled in his seat and rejoined the party. I could see the marina sign a few blocks ahead. A red traffic light slowed my treasure-seeking expedition. At the light I took in the area for possible escape routes and ambush points. The traffic lights were set on 35 mph timers. One mile per hour over or under that speed and a law abiding citizen would catch red lights at every intersection. I wasn't in that category today. Preserving my life was more important than a traffic citation. When the light turned green I pushed the accelerator, eager to get to the undisclosed slip number. I drove the Crown Victoria right by the entrance of the marina. Phil looked out of the window and back at me and asked:.

"What are you doing? That was the entrance. Where are you going?"

I ignored him.

"How often do you come here, Phil?"

"Once or twice a week."

"Ever had any of your clandestine meetings here?"

"No." He answered sarcastically.

"Are you sure?"

"Yes."

I didn't expect him to tell me the truth. I continued driving looking around for dubious vehicles or persons. Most people would be in shorts and flip-flops riding beach-cruiser bikes or driving convertible cars. Any sign of a black van or sedan and Eduardo had sent his soldiers for the same prized possession I was after and to make sure my tree of life died branchless. I drove a few more blocks but didn't see anything out of the ordinary. I made a U-turn and headed back to the entrance. Driving through to the parking lot I heard the newborn man say: "Slip number 32."

I didn't acknowledge or say thank you. When we parked he looked at me, holding his hands up as if to say *are you going to take these off?* I got out of the car and walked around to his side. He could barely stand up straight. His right foot was still swollen from playing this little piggy went to the market. The expensive loafer was untied and he limped as we walked to slip number 32. The night wasn't too warm; it was pleasant. It was quiet by the docks and not an empty slip in sight. Clearly the deteriorated economy hadn't affected this part of the world. Most of the slip numbers were faded and needed repainting. I didn't know what a Mangusta 80 looked like but when I saw the painted letters of "Bar None" I figured we were at Slip number 32.

"Is this your despicable piece of fiberglass?"

"You don't see the slip number?"

"Maybe in your next life you should be a comedian."

Slapping a man was the ultimate insult. I had no respect for him or his repentance. I slapped him across his prickly face and asked the question again.

"Yes this is my yacht."

Even at the obvious end of his life he remained an asshole. The luxurious watercraft had a small cipher lock. I asked for the code.

"You don't know it? You know so much about me."

"Please, no small talk, just the code please."

Standing there waiting for the entry code, I heard someone walking. I pulled out the Bersa and chambered a round. I looked and saw an older gentlemen a few slips down with his small dog going into his water sanctuary. He didn't pay me and the greedy prisoner any attention. He and Phil both part of the same marina club fraternity but certainly no brotherly love between them. Just shared paid for space for their big boy toys.

"The code please?" I asked.

"3275."

I entered the code and turned the small knob to obtain my prize. I don't easily get impressed but the interior was immaculate. The water beast had 14 foot cream color seat benches with blue pillows and marble stationery tables on top of shiny steel poles. I saw a 32-inch flat screen TV and a Sony DVD/CD player. The windows were beveled, with various designs, but you could see outside. I could see the captain's area was made of fine leather and the LED display was the latest in technology. I was certain below deck was just as impeccable but I wasn't at the annual boat show listening to a guided tour.

"Okay where is it?"

"Can I get a drink?"

"When you tell me where the crackerjack prize is."

Empty Soul for Hire

"Now's who's the comedian?"

I stared intensely at him and didn't respond. He pointed his head towards the front of what his high paid retainer fee had gotten him. I hope it was worth it. I looked but didn't see anything that wet my whistle.

"Stop playing games Phil. Remember you're a newborn man. How soon you forget."

"I didn't forget, look at the last cushion by the mini fridge and lift it."

I lifted the last cushion and there was a flat panel on it with a small latch. I slid the latch to open the panel and revealed two JVC CD cases that had the name Banderas on each. I opened each case. The CDs inside didn't have any writing on them.

"What's on them?" I asked

"What every drug lord wants!" he said with confidence.

"Enough riddles, damn you. Just tell me."

"When you find a laptop or computer you'll know what's on them. Now I need a drink?"

I motioned towards the wet bar for him to pollute his soul further with premium libations. He spotted the Macallan Scotch 18-year malt and wrestled to open the bottle, while I enjoyed the plush interior of the rich and shameless. Phil lifted his hands to show me the zip ties around his wrists.

"Make it work the best you can, counselor. I'm not cutting the zip ties."

While he battled with the bottle to get it open, I pulled out my cell and sent a text message to my business associate.

SMS—Call me

Waiting for my phone to ring I looked at the legal beagle struggle to pour his poison. He turned the glass up and managed to consume the expensive scotch in one long gulp. I wondered what he thought as he stood at his elegant bar drinking his last drink and breathing his last few breaths. Was he replaying all of the events that led up to this baneful moment? Was he thinking about all of the school plays, ballet recitals, track meets, graduations, weddings and other significant events of his daughter's lives he wouldn't be part of? He'd never be a grandfather? What was the last thing he told his family before he departed his home 3 days ago to 100 North Tampa. Had he told them he loved them? Or was he like the average American, disrespecting old man time promising he'd get around to it or thinking they knew already. Precious moments and unique opportunities; all lost at the hands of arrogance and greed. Stardom had choked the middle-age biracial man before me and turned him into a fame seeker instead of a defender of innocence. Instead of enjoying the fruits of his tree, he provided materialistic stand-ins and made hefty donations to private schools. Thoughts of my own branchless tree consumed me and sympathy for the loser had me in a head lock.

Eduardo was calling again or at least I thought it was him under the unknown caller alias. I still didn't answer. I wasn't in this war. As soon as I heard back from my associate I was either going to put Phil out of his misery or leave him alive at Slip 32. Either way I would have the Gulfstream jet wheels up within the hour. This mission was coming to an end very soon. I hadn't heard a good story in a while so I asked Phil to tell me his.

"What made you do it?" I asked him.

He didn't answer but continued looking at the floor of his luxurious water taxi. I didn't repeat my question. Maybe he didn't feel the things I thought he should feel and was happy with the decisions he had made.

"You ever had dreams?" he asked

"Sure. But what you're dealing with right now is more of a nightmare."

"It's easy to judge when you're holding the metal."

"Metal or not, you chose to play both sides my friend. Wasn't Banderas' blood money enough?"

"We're friends now?" he asked sarcastically.

"Hardly, bad choice of words."

"I guess it wasn't. I got tired of them paying me whenever they felt like it and whatever they felt like paying. Meanwhile they wanted instant results."

"So Eduardo's people sent a same day Western Union and the blood in your veins pumped faster?"

"What do you care? You're a hired killer. I'm sure you get your tender upfront. I doubt you'd understand my boredom of being a defense attorney for small collar crime?"

"So it was the fame you wanted? To be on the news and the front page of papers as the attorney who represented the Colombian drug lord? Reading your profile I thought you were a smarter man than the one standing before me."

"I'm sorry. I do believe killing is forbidden in the Good Book."

"And so is stealing. You know what? It's really too late for introductions. Sorry I asked the question."

"Do you think I can speak to my daughters?"

"I have no idea. You know Eduardo better than I do and what he's capable of doing."

"Has he called?"

"Several times."

I had to interrupt our belated meet and greet to answer the call from my associate. "Yeah."

"Did you obtain the CDs from Phil's yacht?"

"I did."

"Did you check them?"

"No I wasn't aware I needed to."

"Did this Eduardo clown called back?"

"He's called a few times but I didn't answer. I'm sure he's already killed the witnesses so I didn't see the point of hearing anymore storytelling."

"And Phil?"

"He's standing right here looking pitiful."

"Kill him and get back to L.A. as soon as you can."

"What about Eduardo?"

"We will discuss him later. Your work is done there. Send your usual confirmation text and I will reply with mine."

The phone hung up before I could respond. Normally that wouldn't bother me but this job had become more than just a normal hit. A

Empty Soul for Hire

small portion of it had become personal to me. Although I didn't want to hear the bilingual goon's voice, I was worried about the attorney's daughters. The thoughts of them not having a fair chance bothered me. Every daughter needed her father. Without him, they would most likely grow into women with inner fears of abandonment and emotional baggage. Every time the man in their life would walk out the door to work, or the grocery store, or to get a tank of gas, they'd cringed on the couch or in the bed and wonder if he was coming back. They would run from one relationship to the next looking for what their Daddy never gave them. At the same time not knowing exactly what was missing. This bothered me because I knew as long as I stayed in this business I would never fully commit to anyone and have them bear my fruits. I would continue following the world's anthem of safe sex, not for prevention or the spread of HIV but instead not to infect another life with my demonic seeds. My life wasn't Ward Cleaver's life in "Leave It to Beaver" and as much as I thought I could change, my unfed appetite hungered for the sight of death and not new birth. I was one transaction away from being considered a loyal customer of the in and outcall industry. I was pathetic; I needed the same medicated assistance Mrs. Bach would need.

Phil was looking at me as I held my cell phone in one hand and the foreign made peacemaker in the other. His look told the story I had inquired about earlier, from beginning to end. I believe the man standing before me felt remorse for his greedy actions; he truly wanted a second chance. A chance to be a real father to his children instead of the absent financial giver he'd been, and a loving husband to his single-parent wife. Did he think it would end this way? My subconscious got the best of me at Slip number 32.

"Phil let me ask you something?"

"What? Another judgmental observation?"

"Have you always been so arrogant?"

"Is that your question?"

I smiled at him but didn't respond.

"What is your question?"

"How much did you put away?"

"Are you going to rob me now?"

"Not hardly; just curious."

"All total probably about six million."

"Really?"

"Surprised?"

"I guess I am."

"Changed your mind about robbing me?"

"Your arrogance is beyond this world. If this was about your money I would have taken it a long time ago."

"Then why are you asking?"

"Call me crazy, but I actually thought about letting you go free and giving you another chance. Can I trust you to take your riches and disappear?"

"What about my family?"

"You weren't thinking about them before."

"I'm a reborn man remember?"

"Are you really?"

"I am indeed and I want nothing more to do with this life. I'd be happy working at a Walmart in North Dakota."

"And how would you hide six million in North Dakota?"

"In the mattress. And I'd sleep comfy on it every night."

"And you'd be alright wearing non-designer clothes and shoes from Payless? And drive a car that got more than 16 miles a gallon? I don't see it."

"Trust me. I could after all of this."

My mind continued to play the good deeds game with me. Quick images of his daughters flashed in my mind, and his wife sitting in her weekly therapy sessions and taking Prozac on a daily basis just to get through the day. Perhaps I'm feeling this way because I saw his wife and one of his daughters. Normally I apprehended countless losers like him while they were solo. I didn't dig into their personal lives. This was all Phil's fault. I blamed him for rationalizing my emotional detachment. I took a deep breath and raised the Bersa.

"So this is it?" he asked

I nodded silently. The more we talked the more I'd continue to rationalize giving him another chance, which I knew in the end I couldn't explain to my business associate. Phil's cell phone rang. It was Eduardo. My patience for interruptions had worn thin. I answered and asked: "What now?"

"Why are you so uptight amigo?"

"Eduardo, no small talk."

"I've called you several times."

"I was busy."

"Do you still have Phil?"

"What does it matter? It's not like you haven't destroyed his wife and done God knows what to his daughters. I'm sure the witnesses are no longer breathing citizens."

I tried to make it seem like I didn't care.

"Well stated."

"Can Phil talk to his children?"

"Maybe that can be arranged."

"Yes or no? It's a simple question."

I heard him say some Spanish words and a lot of rustling around on his end. I looked at Phil and he looked happy after hearing of his children. Eduardo came back to the phone.

"Amigo."

"I'm here."

"Where's the greedy attorney?"

I walked over and put the phone up to Phil's ear and told Eduardo he was on the phone. Phil said hello. The sophisticated bean eater immediately started cursing at Phil. I snatched the phone away and told him: "He's supposed to be talking to his girls."

"Mind your own business amigo."

"Either put the children on or I'm disconnecting."

After I said the word "disconnecting" I realized I hadn't connected the scrambler to Phil's cell phone. Damn it. I looked at Phil and the sight of him made me ill.

Empty Soul for Hire

"His children, Eduardo."

"They're right here amigo."

"Put them on the phone now."

I heard the youngest one say "Daddy". I put the phone up to Phil's ear; he began professing his love and saying everything would be alright. The tears were streaming down his face, and I felt his pain. I thought of the last time I heard my own father's voice before he passed away. I was still in the Army and my leadership wouldn't approve my leave to go home. I believe at that very moment is when my fiery was born. I told Phil in a whispering voice to wrap up the conversation. He said his final words of "I love you" to his daughters and I took the phone back. I could hear Eduardo's stinky breath.

"Thanks for the kind gesture;" I said.

"No problem amigo. Do you think his yacht has enough fuel to let you escape?"

He had tracked me down. I had to either give Phil another chance or send him to his savior of choice. I didn't say anything else to Eduardo and threw the cell on the comfy bench. I took three steps back and pointed my weapon at Phil. He was still crying. If I didn't tune him out; I was going to run right past him and leave him for Eduardo's soldiers. Then I'd have more explaining to do, something I wasn't good at. I closed my eyes for a few seconds and when I reopened them I squeezed the trigger. Two hollow points to his chest and one to the center of his forehead. He fell back into the polished cabinetry and the yacht's interior had a new look of biracial blood splattered across its expensive bench cushions and windows.

SMS—JOB COMPLETE

My business associate's reply didn't come immediately like it normally does.

Twenty Four

I don't think Miriam's phone rang a full ring before she answered loudly and overexcited about my date with Khan.

"So girl how was it?" she asked

"Oh my goodness, are you kidding me? You act like this is the first man I've ever dated."

"Well it *has* been a while. So give me details."

"It was nice."

"That's details? What happened at game night? Were his friends cool? Did they think you two were a couple? What did you guys do after game night? Did you get the overdue maintenance service? Is he a good kisser? Come on girl, tell me."

This is precisely why I didn't want to call Miriam right away. She's always over the top with the questions and assumptions. I'm beginning to think she lives vicariously through me and my dull life even though she has a man. I let her go on with her questions while I read the title caption on the Lifetime movie coming on. A suspense thriller about a haunted house by Anne Rice was coming on. Miriam hadn't come up for air.

"Jordan, are you there?" she asked

"I'm here."

"What's up? Did you hear my questions?"

"Miriam, do you think I'm that fast to jump in bed with a man?" I asked, annoyed.

"Oh please, spare me the message from the church service you're watching on TV. This is *me*, so what's up?"

I was further annoyed.

"Game night was nice. His friends were cool, no pressure about being a couple. We went to the Seabird Lounge afterwards. At the end of the night he was still a gentleman."

"A gentleman? What the heck does that mean?"

"It means he didn't force anything and I didn't play myself cheap."

"No kiss. Nothing?"

"Miriam are you for real right now?"

"As a heart attack. You didn't give him any last night? I'm really surprised."

When someone says they're "really" surprised about something, it normally means they *expected* a different response or action from you. Miriam was really pushing my buttons this morning with her demeaning tone and interrogating questions. Khan was attractive and all, but so were a lot of the others I had trusted only to be disappointed. I was doing things differently this time around. It's a shame my best friend wasn't onboard with that.

"Miriam, we kissed at the end of the evening and that was it."

"Girl I know the rose man was in the lounge. Khan didn't buy you a rose?"

"No! And I'm glad he didn't. Last I knew, red roses were a token of love and we certainly don't love each other; we don't even know each other."

"Yeah, yeah, I'll let you get back to your Sunday televised church service. You're funny Jordan."

"No you're the funny one! Have a good day!"

I hung up before she could say any more belittling things to me; started watching the movie on Lifetime. Miriam had irritated me so much I couldn't get into the movie. Damn! I got up and started going through old magazines to put in the recycle bin on Tuesday. Several back issues of *Essence, Travel Leisure* and *O* that I either had read or hadn't and probably wouldn't at this point. I'm sure there were new trendy items and columns of advice by now. I needed to get myself together before I met up with Khan because I didn't hide things well. It wouldn't be fair to him to show up in a bad mood, and canceling for no real reason would be rude. I retreated to my bathroom to take a shower. The hot water and steam gives me calmness and helps my mind refocus.

When I got out of the shower I looked in my closet for something to wear. I really felt like wearing jogging pants today instead of jeans. Unfortunately I didn't have anything that wouldn't draw undue attention to my rear end. I tried on two different ones and looked at myself in my standing mirror. Couldn't run from it; I had my mommy's sexy buns. Maybe if I wore briefs instead of a thong it would help. Otherwise, my backside would jiggle like Jello and I didn't want Khan doing the impression of the guy from the jello pudding commercials. I chose my navy blue jogging suit with a white t-shirt and got ready to head out. My ringtone "Independent Women" sang out loud on my cell phone. Miriam had sent a text message. I hope she wasn't still tripping about my date with Khan. I didn't check it right away I kept getting dressed. I didn't know how traffic would be this afternoon so I left out to give myself enough time. If I arrive early; I'll stop by the little shops by the airport to kill some time.

The 405 freeway was jam-packed as I expected it to be. I love the City of Angels, but this traffic gets old. Against my better judgment, I checked Miriam message. *Jordan I apologize for earlier.* That was nice but she should've called and apologized. It would have felt more sincere than a text message. It made me feel like she didn't really mean it. I'll call her later. That's my girl. The traffic broke after the 10 interchange but I didn't have too much time to spare. When I got to the El Segundo exit it was 3:40 PM and the street traffic was heavy. God please don't let me be late. Most of the drivers were tourists trying to get back to the car rental return. Sitting at the traffic light at Nash and El Segundo I received a text from Khan letting me know he was at the movies and had bought the tickets already. He said I could buy the popcorn and drinks. I laughed to myself. After I found a parking space and I walked as fast as I could without sweating. Some knucklehead blasting his music tried to talk to me.

"Hey cutie, can I go jogging with you?"

I ignored him. When I got outside I could see Khan standing by the windows where you buy the tickets. He saw me walking towards him and smiled. He had a nice smile. I didn't feel so bad when I saw he had on a jogging suit as well. We embraced quickly when I walked up to him.

"Hi Jordan, I see both of us wanted to relax today."

I smiled. "Yeah I didn't want to wear jeans."

"I hear you. I didn't even shave."

"Did you shower?" I asked

"Do I stink?" he asked with a smirk

"No! I just thought men did the three S's and didn't think you guys did one without the others."

He laughed and said "let's go inside the movie." When we walked up to the concession stand, I was certain I saw my ex-boyfriend but he didn't see me. I was glad he didn't because I wasn't ready to go down memory lane or pretend we were still friends. Talk about bad choices. He fooled some of the best including me. This dude had the premium business cards, knew the right things to say, and was knowledgeable about world events, but what he didn't have was a real job. He was unemployed and still living off his mother. No degree, not even an associate degree. That was a long year I wish I could forget.

Khan pulled out money to pay for the snacks but I reminded him I was doing that today. This was agreed to earlier. By the time the movie was over it was dark outside and the little plaza had liven up with couples, groups, and first date meetings. It was a little chilly but nice out. I saw Khan reach for my hand as we starting walking. My uncontrollable subconscious led my hand to his warm hands. He looked at me and smiled.

"Did you like the movie?" he asked.

"It was pretty good, one of the better ones."

"Yeah I didn't think I would like the new James Bond but he's actually pretty good."

"Of course he's no Sean Connery but he's good."

"Are you hungry?"

"Sure, what did you have in mind."

"PF Changs."

"Oh yes I love their lettuce wraps and the egg-drop soup. How long do you think the wait is though? I see a lot of people waiting."

"Only one way to find out."

We both forgot we had on jogging suits clearly. As we approached the door, I felt the stares and heard the low whispers. Everyone was casually dressed. Oh well, this wasn't a planned dinner. We just left the movies.

"It's an hour wait or first available at the bar. I was thinking the bar, given the way we're dressed, or would you mind getting it to go and eat at my place?" he asked cautiously.

There it was; the invite to his place. Do I accept, or decline and pick up a bite to eat on my way home? I looked at the bar area. The Clippers were playing the Heat so I doubt if anyone was leaving anytime soon. Another group of folks walked in and the Pacific Ocean breeze blew in my inside erotic voice and she started trying to sway me. *Go ahead girl, go to his place. Have a little Asian cuisine and get your tires balanced and rotated. We can work on the check engine light later. But get a little maintenance before your work week starts.* Before I knew it, I told Khan to order take-out and let's go to his place. After he placed the order, he ordered a beer and asked me if I wanted anything. I ordered a Rum Manhattan.

"Thank you for accepting the invite." He said.

"No problem. I didn't want to wait an hour to eat and it probably would be that long anyplace else as well."

"True, true. So do you have a busy week this week?"

"I don't think so. But you never know with the bank. Who knows what changes the branch manager wants to implement. What about you?"

"Not too bad, typical week in the education world."

"Do you love what you do, or is it just to pay the bills?"

"I love being an educator. It gives me joy attempting to make a difference in someone's life. I wish more teachers felt the same. Everything you do in life can't be about the money. A deep passion should be inside every person to do what they love and not just do it for money. But hey I'm not trying to give you the Sunday evening sermon."

"Hallelujah! I heard the morning sermon on TV."

"Really? Who do you listen to you?"

"It was an inside joke."

"Oh okay."

The waiter brought our order to where we were standing and Khan closed out the tab. When we stepped back outside, it seemed chillier than before.

"Where did you park?" Khan asked

"I'm on the 3rd level."

"I'm in the valet. I can give you a ride to your car and then you can follow me."

"Thanks that would be nice."

Khan opened the passenger door for me when the valet attendant pulled up in his vehicle. When we got to my vehicle, Khan asked if I was sure I wanted to go his place?

"Yes I'm sure; how far do you live from here?" I asked

"Off the 405 by the old Fox Hills mall."

"Okay, I'm right behind you."

Traffic wasn't too bad on the freeway and we were at Khan's place in no time. I followed him into the parking garage of his complex and parked next to his car. I asked him if my car would be towed for parking here. He laughed and said no. As we walked to the entry door I could smell the Chinese food but my attention was really on Khan's gluteus maximus. The jogging suit he had on showed how tight it was. Oh my God, why am I looking at this man like that? *That's it girl check out the mechanic before you let him under the hood. He looks certified to me, pull into his bay.* The elevator bell snapped me out of my mental foreplay. His apartment was on the top floor of the complex. When he opened the door of his apartment I was immediately met with a nice aroma from a reed diffuser. His living room was nicely furnished with a chocolate leather sofa, matching chair, and two floor lamps. I could see a few issues of the *Savoy* magazine on his coffee table and the Sunday paper. On one wall he had a flat screen television mounted with the shelving for his stereo equipment. The other walls had beautiful paintings. I had seen one of the limited prints by L'roy Campbell. I couldn't see his bedroom or bathroom because the doors were closed. His kitchen counter had bar stools and two place settings. I had to admit his place was decorated classy. Thank God I didn't see a video game console with video game cartridges everywhere; a grown man for a change. Khan interrupted my housing inspection

"Would you like to eat at the kitchen counter or on the couch?" he asked.

"You eat in your living room?"

"Sometimes."

"We can eat at the kitchen counter. I don't want your leather sofa smelling like egg drop soup."

"It's just a couch, but as you wish."

Empty Soul for Hire

    Surprisingly, after we finished eating I wasn't ready to leave. I felt relaxed and comfortable. I watched Khan clean up the leftover food and put the plates in his dishwasher. The t-shirt he had on revealed his physique better than I remember from the coffee shop and unconsciously I licked my lips but he didn't see me. I could tell he followed the advice column of WebMd regarding physical activity and did cardio four or five times a week for at least 30 minutes. The sound of his manly voice snapped me out of my trance.

    "Would you like to watch some TV or is music fine?" he asked.

    "Can we see what's on TV?"

    "Sure. Can I get you something to drink?"

    "What do you have?"

    "Juice, a few brews, and some alcohol in the cabinet."

    "Let me have a beer."

    "Coming right up."

    "Thank you."

    "Anything in particular you want to watch?"

    "You probably wouldn't want to watch that?"

    "Oh yeah? What did you have in mind?"

    "I normally watch Lifetime all day on Sundays."

    "You're right. I'll pass on the Lifetime. What about a basketball game?"

    "Okay."

The Spurs were playing the team that moved from New Jersey to Brooklyn. I could tell Khan was an avid sports fan because the communication pretty much ended after he tuned into the game. He would say something quickly during the commercials or time outs. Maybe watching the game wasn't such a good idea. I wanted some attention. When the next commercial came on I got his attention when I asked:

"When was your last serious relationship?"

I could tell my question caught him off guard. He put his hands on his knees and exhaled as if I'd dropped a ton on bricks on him. His eyes were straight ahead on the TV; then he turned towards me and said: "It was over a year ago. What about you?"

"Longer than that for me."

"It's hard out here, you know?"

"Please! I know exactly what you mean, but men have it easy."

"How's that?"

"Nevermind. I shouldn't have said that."

"No! Speak freely."

"No it's okay."

"Look Jordan, I'm really into you but I don't want to seem desperate. But at the same time, I need to let you know how I feel. I'm not worried about being too cool or a soft guy. I'm just being real. I could text you every free moment I had during the day and call you as soon as the last student left my classroom. But as a man I do have some dignity and I would think as a woman if a decent man was showing her admiration and being a gentleman then she'd be real with him instead of acting half interested."

"Khan, how do I know you're all those things? We've only been on three dates. Well four, if you count today. I am attracted to you and think you have what I'm looking for in a man. No offense, but I promised myself the next guy that crossed my path I would take it slow. I hope you can understand that."

"Jordan I do understand but honestly I don't think you should put a time clock on your emotions. Chemistry is the ability to draw attention or something that draws attention. Aren't we drawn to each other?"

Oh my God! What he just said sounded so sexy. In L.A. a lot of men had tons of lines they ran on women to get what they wanted. After they got *it* a few times, then the games and excuses prevailed. I was looking at Khan intensely with intimate thoughts stirred by what my ears had just heard. His look was innocent and devious at the same time. Lord, don't let this man be a waste of my time.

Twenty Five

I **took one last** look at the dead attorney before grabbing his cell phone and leaving Slip number 32. When I got up on the dock I saw the old man from earlier peeking out the windows of his modern ark. I looked at him and kept a steady pace back to the Crown Vic. I pulled out my cell phone and called Stratos Jet Charter services to inquire about an immediate departure back to the Pacific Standard Time side of the world. The next available reservationist of the premiere charter service answered in delightful voice but I couldn't appreciate her welcoming greeting. I was rudely interrupted by the sound of gunfire near my feet ricocheting off the concrete. I dove behind a parked car to see where this intrusive introduction was coming from. I saw four burly men aiming automatic weapons in my direction. I pulled out my peacemaker to return the greeting and let them know their presence wasn't appreciated. The Crown Vic was a few cars away along with the rest of my arming associates. My piece in hand was good but I would need some reinforcement soon to respond properly to this unexpected meeting. My cell phone buzzed. It was the charter service calling me back. Technology had given businesses and consumers the capability to dial back drop calls and hang ups. I couldn't be rude and not give my new acquaintances my undivided attention. I let the call go to voicemail. As one of the men ran toward to me I clipped him in one of his kneecaps. As he fell the nerves in his fingers caused his weapon to spray bullets in every direction. I ducked under the car I was hiding behind. He lay there on the ground screaming out in pain for his Jehovah and cursing me. When the sounds of repetitive bullets stopped I took aim and sent him my best wishes; one hollow-point to his greasy dome. My sincere farewell got the attention of the other three. I saw one of them talking on a radio, most likely calling for more blazing fire. I didn't have the time or the equipment to continue this heated engagement; I took off for the Crown Vic as the bullets kept searching for my flesh in the parking lot. I started my getaway car and shifted to drive and floored it. My new friends retreated to a dark colored van and pursued me. I couldn't take this meeting to the airport or the hotel. Doing so would raise other questions that I didn't want to answer. That reminded me I still hadn't received a reply to my text from my associate.

Before I hit the Courtney Causeway I took a few small streets to try and end this redundant meeting nicely or deadly. At this point I just wanted to get back to Los Feliz Hills, hand off these two discs, and relax for a few minutes. Phil's stubbornness wasn't expected and I needed to recoup from it. I also wanted to speak to Jordan and hopefully redeem myself and take her out. My thoughts were readjusted when the driver side mirror was shot off and the back window shattered. I made a quick right turn down a one-way street and then another quick right. I got out and popped the trunk and pulled out the A2 automatic weapon. I could hear the engine of the van heading my way but they weren't on the same street. I got back inside the manufactured Lincoln and waited to see if they would pass the small street or find me. When I saw the dark van zoom by I shifted to reverse. Now I was chasing them. I pushed the gas pedal to the floor and rammed the back of the van twice. The back door of the van swung open and I was met with gunfire. I swerved to the left as the bullets continued redesigning my second getaway car. Smoke appeared from the hood and one of my tires had been hit. I needed to swerve back to enjoy this new version of the game chicken. The gunmen unloaded their clips at the car and me. My daredevil driving skills kept me alive as the bullets maintained a connection with the Crown Vic. When I got to the right of the dark van I let the A2 introduce herself with ten fast rounds. I hit one of the ruffians sent to end my branchless tree of life and he fell out of the van. I wondered if the current administration's health plan was

Empty Soul for Hire

in his favor as the tires crushed his diseased protoplasm. I tried to catch up to the van's passenger side but the driver kept swerving to the right to prevent that. I floored the gas pedal and got close to the front of the van but the Indy 500 driver wasn't making this easy. My mode of transportation couldn't keep up this game of chicken. I shot the front right tire hoping the driver would lose control; the van swerved but his skills were impeccable. We passed through another intersection and my pole position changed. I saw the driver's face; his olive oil skin tone and hair full of Hair Cuttery products confirmed his employer—Eduardo aka Solderota Cartel. I reached over to the passenger seat and pulled out a grenade. My thoughts drifted for a split second and Phil's daughters flooded my frontal. Should I keep the driver alive and wait for the anticipated call from Eduardo and attempt an exchange? Those girls needed a fair chance. Their demise at the expense of an overzealous attorney, their father, just wasn't right and didn't sit well with me. I looked at the driver again and considered his expiration date. He was a dime a dozen to Eduardo and easily replaced but the two discs, I bet, were priceless. I pulled the pin and threw the grenade through the window and slammed on the brakes. Seconds later I watched the van explode into flames. The dead attorney's cell phone rang—great timing on the unknown caller's part. I let it ring until it reached the maximum number of rings before the voicemail answered the call. The caller didn't leave a message instead they redialed and the phone rang again. I didn't feel like chit-chatting at the moment so I ignored the calls as the caller continued redialing. I did my own redialing to the chartered jet services to finish my return flight request. The reservationist wasn't as pleasant as the last person. I extended a pleasant greeting but she didn't return the gesture. Her voice was stern and to the point.

"Is your flight request one way, roundtrip, domestic, or international?" she asked.

"It's the return leg of a roundtrip."

"What's your last name?"

"How are you today?"

The phone was silent. I waited to see if the parsimonious worker would respond. No such luck.

"Goodman"

"Thank you. What day would you like to return to Hawthorne, California from Tampa, Florida?"

"The soonest available please."

"One moment please."

At least she said please this time. She came back on the line in the same austere tone.

"A crew can be available in two hours. Will that work for you?"

I returned the same rancor in my response.

"What other choice do I have?"

I heard her sigh heavily with much attitude. Just thought I'd share a little of the wealth.

"Shall I book the return?" she asked curtly.

"What time is the departure?" I responded, just as impolite.

She could dish it but didn't like being on the receiving end. I heard her sigh again then she finally answered.

"Your flight would depart two hours after I booked the leg."

"Put me in a seat then."

"Are you familiar with the private terminal at the Tampa International Airport?"

Empty Soul for Hire

"I am."

"Do you need transportation to the airport?"

"I do not."

"You are confirmed to depart the Tampa International Airport at 10:30 this evening, arriving in Hawthorne at 11:00 PM, Pacific Standard Time. Thank you for choosing Stratos, you confirmation number is the same from your original booking. I hope I have answered all of your questions. Do you have any questions for me?"

After she read her company formatted response to me I just hung up the phone. I was tired of playing the discourteous game with her. That really wasn't my nature. Besides throughout the whole conversation, the other cell phone rang incessantly from the unknown caller, and that annoyed me more than the crude reservationist.

When I crossed the causeway back into Tampa I called my local contact and told him I would be departing in a couple of hours.

"What should I do with the local assets provided?" I asked.

"What condition is the Lincoln in?" he asked nonchalantly.

"Got into a game of chicken" I responded hesitantly.

"No problem! And the other things?"

"Honestly didn't do an inventory. I walked into the O.K. Coral in Clearwater."

"You straight?"

Physically I was fine but mentally I had dubious thoughts in my head and still unanswered questions and no reply to my text message from my business associate. The non-response was very odd of him, which gave me more unsettling apprehension. What was on these CDs? Phil didn't volunteer to tell me and I didn't want to open them on any of my personal electronic gadgets. Where was a Kinkos when you needed one? I answered my loyal colleague after my inner thoughts subsided.

"I'm good to go."

"Okay. Just leave Crown Vic and everything left over in long-term parking. Do you need anything else?"

"No. As usual your services were beyond compare. Send your invoice as soon as it's ready my friend."

"You know it's never been about the money. Have a safe flight back and keep in touch."

Before I could respond the call ended and my contact was gone. Unlike Eduardo, my usual contacts weren't into intimate telephone foreplay. We had a confidential relationship. They took my orders with no questions asked and I returned them the same courtesies. I pulled into the long-term parking garage and parked the Lincoln. I grabbed my personal gear out of the trunk and looked around the garage for any more undesired introductions. Once I close the trunk and head to the terminal I will be at the mercy of an undertrained airport security guard leaving my chances of survival nil. After surveying the immediate area for what seemed like an eternity, I closed the trunk and left the keys under the backseat floor mat and proceeded to the terminal. As I got closer to the door I could see the elevators inside but I heard the sounds of screeching wheels so I quickly turned around to see if Eduardo's henchmen had found me. I saw a man and woman in a Honda Accord searching for a space to park. I exhaled and continued inside. When I got to the main terminal it was chaotic, just as I remembered it. I didn't waste time. I found the sign for the private terminal and walked in that direction. My head and eyes were on a swivel as I made my way through the general population terminal. I really don't think I could get used to this way of travel again. After the doors to the private terminal closed behind me, the immediate quietness was back. The lounge in Tampa was nicer but busier than Hawthorne; chartered flights were a dime a dozen here like LAX, which was the main reason I chose Hawthorne, California for my travel needs. The customer service was similar to the quality I received earlier but the terminal wasn't owned by Stratos so I couldn't blame them this time.

I bought some water and sat in the small lounge for Stratos customers. There was an older gentlemen sitting inside reading the *Wall Street Journal* and having a cocktail. We acknowledged one another with the signature gentleman head nod. I sat across from him on the plush sofa. A small-framed woman resembling the terminal employee in Hawthorne came and asked if I would care for a cocktail before takeoff. I politely declined. The liquid poison I yearned for was in Los Feliz Hills. Before leaving she checked on the gentleman across from me. He declined a second drink. I pulled out my cell phone to see if I had missed an incoming text message. I hadn't. Through the glass doors I saw a familiar body structure paying for some concessions. The person was about 5 ft 2 in, light mocha complexion, and had long hair. I shook my head in disbelief but when she turned around and flung her long mane away from her face, my skepticism was confirmed. It was Carnival Cutie. Her direction of walk led her through the glass doors of the Stratos small lounge. Damn, maybe her profession was just as profitable as mine but safer. I shook those considering thoughts quickly. I couldn't show up at the door of someone Earth Kitt's age for an outcall. That guy with the funny laugh from "Saturday Night Live" had that age group under control. Our eyes met as she walked through the door and she remembered her recent client with the nice taste. I didn't make a scene or request an on the spot refund. I stayed seated. Her walked slowed a little, but like Hollyweird's finest actresses she got back into her part. She sat next to the older gentlemen across from me. He asked her if she found what she was looking for. Her innocent eyes slightly looking at me answered her current client with the better taste than me. I did my best not to make her feel uncomfortable or give the richer gift giver any sign of affiliation. Although he knew there was nothing monogamous between him and the outcall profile he was taking to an undisclosed location, this wasn't the time to discuss my customer service complaint. I looked at my watch; the second hand was moving slower than ever, it seemed. At least I knew we weren't boarding the same aircraft and this perplexing situation would be over soon.

The elephant remained at large in the small lounge as three strangers with similar interests waited to board their jet fuel guzzlers. One of the strangers heading home, the other with akin interests traveling with the well paid for passenger to an exotic location I'm certain. I felt the lounge shake as the large creature started to leave the room when I heard *Mr. Goodman please proceed to Gate 1 for departure.* Following my announcement the automated voice said *Mr. Cavanaugh and Ms. Taylor please proceed to Gate 2 for departure.* The richer gift giver and his gift recipient stood up and proceeded to their gate. I stayed seated until they were out of the immediate area. I saw them waiting at the door of Gate 2 and Ms. Taylor looked back at me just before entering the humid air with her latest gift giver. Her eyes told me she was unhappy with her line of work and wanted to be rescued. I thought about Phil's daughters and how their traumatic experience would affect them. What influence had Phil left in their mind other than his generous tithes and offerings to their educational institutions and lavish vacations? How would they see their mother after hearing her painful moans and screams; watching man after man and not their father have undesired sex with their mother? What traumatic or life changing event made Ms. Taylor aka Carnival Cutie put a pleasure pleasing profile on the World Wide Web for gifts? Had her father abandoned or abused her? Did her mother not teach her how to be a lady? Or did her mother show her how not to love and now she was numb to commitment and emotional connection; just a financial connection at a lofty gift rate per hour? Had a man from a previous relationship showed her the love she didn't receive growing up, only to use it to his advantage at the expense of her mental stability and degrading her body with countless gift givers? The gift givers furthered the problem with slush fund accounts their better half would never find out about until he was free from his sins and the estate planner revealed his assets. I didn't have a better half and no offspring to leave my blood money to; I was still a contributor to the problem though. The automated announcer broke

Empty Soul for Hire

my distant stare at one of Brazil's good girl gone bad forever. *Mr. Goodman please report to Gate 1 for departure.* I grabbed my duffle bag and headed to my gate. The doors to Gate 2 closed slowly and so did my thoughts of the lost soul I'd given a gift to myself. Eduardo was still calling a dead person's phone but I had no intentions of answering, so I powered the phone off completely. I pulled out my own cell phone and started typing a text to Jordan. I couldn't type anything other than *Hi Jordan*. I didn't know how to tell her I was now available after killing several people and considering illegally adopting the two little girls of a man I tortured and killed. When I sat down in the soft leather chair on the jet I pulled my phone out again hoping to complete a simple message. One of the flight attendants came to my seat and introduced herself. She asked if she could get me anything before takeoff? I responded with an insulting question: "What do you know about history?"

She smiled and then answered in an Australian accent.

"Excuse me, sir."

"History! What do you know about it?"

"I'm not sure I understand."

"Tell me, who's your favorite king?"

Her smile no longer present and a look of confusion ever present. I wasn't having fun anymore. I was irritated with the wrong person.

"Do you have King Louis XIII cognac on board?" I asked snidely.

Her smile was back. Not because she knew of the king I mentioned but she knew what spirits they had. I never lost eye contact and waited for her response.

"Sir I'm afraid we don't have that on board. Would you like something else instead?"

I smiled unpleasantly and as polite as I could I declined the something else offered. She continued with the standard boarding salutations of what they offered and told me the name of the other flight attendant. My mental responder had shut down after the recent one-sided conversation a few minutes ago. When she completed the chartered flights version of safety before takeoff and beverage service I smiled and looked back at my phone. She returned the smile, turned, and walked away. I can't wait to get to Los Feliz Hills and talk to my favorite King.

SMS—Hi Jordan, I was hoping we could get together soon. I'm finally finished with the project that took longer than I expected.

I heard some of the captain's announcement before I powered my phone off and closed my eyes. I didn't receive a reply from Jordan and still hadn't heard back from my associate. The right side of my head invited a migraine as I began my return leg.

Twenty Six

My eyes remained closed as Khan's lips stay locked with mine and his hands caressed my back. His hands were strong but his touch was soft and relaxing. I felt my body being overtaken and giving in to the chemistry he spoke about. I felt his right hand rubbing and squeezing the outside of my left thigh. My hands felt every muscle in his back and biceps. I felt him pull his lips back from me as if a hired locksmith had entered his apartment to unlock our lustful security breach. His dark eyes were burning through my body with looks of passionate lust and desire. He grabbed my hand and stood up. Facing each other, he came towards my lips again to give the locksmith another opportunity for unlocking service. I felt my own breathing increase and my sexual juices start to flow. I didn't think I was ready for this. We paused for a moment and then Khan led me to his bedroom. Behind one of the closed doors was a black king size bed with a black chest of drawers and two night stands with lamps. Another television was on the wall and I saw a Bose stereo system. I didn't see any family or friends in photo frames, just another magazine and a man's valet on his chest of drawers with assorted manly things. Khan asked if he could get me anything. From the looks of things, I was going to get it in a few minutes. I smiled and told him I was okay. I saw him turn on the stereo system and the sounds of John Coltrane entered the room. I could tell he was into music and loved jazz. When he turned back around his hands touched my shoulders and slid underneath the jogging suit jacket. He slid the jacket off my shoulders and grabbed each sleeve and I agreeably pulled each arm out. His eyes never left my eyes and his smile remain welcoming as his hands continued to undress me. He wasn't in a rush and his touch flowed to my body's yearning. He kissed my neck as he lifted my t-shirt over my head. The warm breeze on my skin got my attention.

"Wait, wait." I said all of a sudden.

"What's wrong?" He replied disappointed.

"Nothing . . . it's just um . . ."

I fumbled with the words to say to him. I knew I wanted to have sex with him, at this point but still wasn't quite sure. I was looking away from him but I felt him looking directly at me waiting for a response. The scent of his flavored Altoid was blowing in my face.

"Jordan."

"Yes."

"Do we need to stop?"

Girl you better not stop this mechanic in the middle of this overdue tune-up. Don't wait until you're stranded on the side of the road and have to call triple A and some overweight man breathing heavy comes to your rescue. Go ahead girl, let him under the hood. My guardian service advisor was wide awake and encouraging me to go through with this encounter. I looked back at Khan and scanned his chiseled body. My lips on their own finally said something.

"Khan, do you have condoms?"

I couldn't tell if he was upset that I had asked or if he was trying to remember in his mind if he had any.

"Yes I do. Are you allergic to a certain kind?"

Empty Soul for Hire

Oh my God, he's really killing me with the kindness.

"No I'm not."

He went to the chest of drawers and opened the top drawer. I saw the black Trojan wrappers he pulled out. That black label meant only one thing—Magnum size. Was he really fit for that condom size or was that a ploy to impress women? Men are normally more discreet when they pull condoms out. At least that's been my *bad* experience. The educator slash part time worker came back publicly displaying the male contraceptive. I smiled at him acknowledging my gratitude for him being responsible. I saw him toss the condoms on the bed and continued undressing me. I reached for his t-shirt to take it off. He let me lift the pima cotton shirt over his head. His chest had no hair and his stomach was muscular like one of the Roman gladiators. He went to lift my sports bra but I asked if I could leave that on for now. He smiled a boyish smile. I could tell he was growing a little impatient. He pulled the drawstring of my jogging pants and I didn't stop him. The two-loop knot came undone with ease and he slid my pants down. He was attentive as he bent down and lifted each leg out. He took off his sweats and I saw his legs reveal the payoff for doing leg lifts and squats. I saw him taking in my body. Damn it, I didn't have on matching bra and panty. Sports bras didn't come with the matching thong. I laughed to myself.

"Jordan, your body is mesmerizing." he said excitedly

"Thank you. You're not half bad yourself."

Our lips met again but this time our bodies touched without the non-American made clothing between us. His skin was smooth but tight. I abruptly pushed him back and looked at his body. He had a look of let down as if I was going to get dressed and leave. I was looking to see if he had any tattoos. Thank God he didn't. I smiled and he smiled back but not for the same reasons as my smile. He led me to the side of the bed and we lay down together. He rubbed my body from head to toe and kissed me softly as he took one of my breasts in his hand. A quick moan escaped my lips and he caressed and kissed my nipple. I reached to grab one of this thighs and to squeeze his tight butt. I could feel his hands easing into my sweet zone. I grabbed his hand for a few seconds and our eyes met awkwardly. I saw him slump his shoulders down in defeat. I stared into his eyes as I let go of his hand. His hand got back on the trail and slid under my panties and his fingers found that fleshy part of me. His fingers began massaging one of the most sensitive areas of a woman's body. Mine was no different. My head turned the opposite way and drifted off. One of my hands went searching for his yet to be determined Magnum-size love pole. The blood in his Roman body was flowing because he was already rock hard by the time my hand reached his love pole. I started stroking his love pole. He grabbed my hand to stop my foreplay action. I turned and looked at him.

"Is everything okay?" I asked surprisingly.

His breathing was a little fast.

"Um ah . . . yeah."

"Are you sure?"

"Yes."

He let go of my hand and I continued stroking the male species ego booster. My love canal's juices were flowing nice at this point and I'm certain the finger he slid inside wouldn't look the same as it did before going inside. The touch of my hand on his manhood didn't tell me he was fit for the condoms he'd pulled out. Educated or not, I knew nothing about penile size or penile enlargement. My love walls would soon perform the evaluation and confirm whether he should continue wasting his money or if I should stop by the drug store to make sure I had the black labels in my nightstand for his visits to my place. Khan started pulling my panties down. I lifted my hips, lending him some assistance and I took off my sports bra. He took off his Hanes underwear and reached for one of the prepackaged black labels. I lay there trying to prepare my mind for this. It had been close to a year since Heaven had been visited other than for my annual checkup. I looked at him, then at his manhood as he tore the black label open. I still couldn't see the snug fit occurring but here we go.

I took one last look to ensure the chances of sexual transmitted diseases were securely prevented. They were and the fit wasn't snug at all. I quickly thought about the Starbuck's worker asking a patron if they needed room for cream with their coffee. There was plenty of room to spare inside the unwrapped black label product. I felt Khan's muscular frame climb on top of me and his hand searching for my wet entrance. His manhood slid inside of me and I felt the in and out movement but my love walls were lonely and screaming for attention. I looked at him put his best efforts to work as I tried to adjust to him. I whispered in his ear, "Take it slow Khan."

"Okay I am baby."

We never did agree on a pace I guess. His idea of slow was fast thrusting against my pelvic area and an occasional kiss. This reminded me of a love scene with the late great Whitney Houston and this guy she gave her loving to. He spent more time brushing his teeth with her toothbrush than he did making love to her. In a matter of seconds he was growling. She was a zoo-keeper and here I was a track and field coach trying to get someone to slow down. My breasts were lonely too. I tried to move my hips with his groove but he was too fast and strong. He had one of my legs in the air and thought he was going deep; surely we were still in the kiddie pool area. When he rose up I asked him if I could get on top. He looked disappointed that I had interrupted his track and field sprint training. But I knew if I had any chance of reaching an orgasm I had to get on top. He grudgingly obliged and lay on his back. When I straddled him his disappointed look hadn't changed and he no longer looked interested. His manhood seemed in the same frame of mind obviously because Mr. Black Label lost some luster. I rubbed the unfilled tip of the condoms against my clit and he was back in the game. I slid him inside and began the adjusted ride. His eyes were closed as my hips swayed back and forth against his false advertised manhood size. I was trying not to focus on that and focus on an orgasm. It was hard not to think about the deception. I grabbed one of my own breasts since the educator wasn't interested in the Anatomy & Physiology lesson. I zoned off into my own world and thought of something to get me to the mountaintop that an old civil rights leader used to speak about. My lustful thoughts reached out to Lance and I smiled. His body wasn't as tight as the one lying here but his male member had my walls swollen and my clit was pulsating from his manly slow stroke. He grooved in and out of my vagina like the Roman Gladiator I thought I had in front of me. His touch was powerful and let me know who had the upper hand. I rode the part time worker from Banana Republic thinking of the mysterious man from Kinkos that replied intermittently to my text messages and called after the old cell phone plan of "non-peak" hours. My body adjusted to the non-intimidating size inside me but my mind had spoken to someone else during the ride. The way I rode Khan made him open his eyes but my eyes were closed now. He tried to grab my hips but I no longer needed his help. I was crossing the finish line of the track meet he had started. I could see the tape drawn across the individual lanes but I had no competition to the left or right of me. I had the thoughts of a mystery man working my body and the check-engine light going dim. I opened my eyes just before I reached the finish line to look at Khan so I wouldn't accidentally give credit to the other mechanic for my tune up. But I thought for a second, men do it all the time. They keep silent so they don't call you someone else they're thinking about. I slowed my groove and closed my eyes again as my body met with the hard orgasm. I moaned a little and exhaled slowly as I lay on the stand in character from my erotic dream. I felt Khan's hands on my back. His average size member lost its luster again. He kissed my ear softly but I was over it at this point. I lay there to not appear rude like men do after they blast their seeds and get up and turn on the TV. He rubbed and squeezed my booty. Now he wants to register for the Anatomy & Physiology class. No thanks, that class is no longer available. Maybe you should look for an online class. I couldn't pretend anymore. I slid off of him and lay next to him. I could feel his eyes on me but he didn't say anything. I kept quiet as well. After a few seconds, I heard him sigh and the sound of the oversized condom coming off. He sat up on the side of the bed for a few seconds, then went to the bathroom. I heard the condom entering the public waste system and then the faucet water. When he came back in the room he asked if I wanted anything to drink. I smiled to myself and felt like I should have gotten a power drink endorsement for the way I performed at this track meet. It's not every day you outlast your partner in this type of sport. Most times you come in second place or dead last while they're out of breath from rudely beating you to the finish line and not even thanking you for your support. I turned over on his defeated field of mischievous play and saw him standing there with his underwear on.

"No thank you." I replied happily.

He turned and left the room. I went back to my happy place and closed my eyes—again.

Twenty Seven

I felt soft hands tapping my shoulders and heard a British accent calling my name trying to wake me from my nightmares. I opened my eyes to see the other flight attendant smiling and informing me that we would be landing soon. I lifted the shade and saw the lighted buildings of downtown L.A. to my right. I could see the Hollywood Park race track lights and hundreds of clear and red lights on the streets and freeways. I thanked the young looking flight attendant.

"Mr. Goodman would you like a hot towel?" she asked sweetly.

"Yes that would be nice, thank you."

"Coming right up."

She turned around and walked to the front of the jet. Unlike the flight attendants on my first leg, She didn't show any shape or curve in her company uniform. I looked back out the window and thought about my drive to Los Feliz Hills and the empty house that awaited me, and what was on the two discs I obtained. I felt the jet descending into the small municipal airport. The flight attendant returned with the hot towel and asked if I would need anything else before landing. I declined.

When the small ground crew met the inbound flight from the humidity capital of the world and the door opened I could feel the cool evening breeze of beautiful Southern California and smell the polluted ocean water from nearby Manhattan Beach. I thanked the higher wage flight attendants as I exited and got in the courtesy golf cart. When I powered my cell phone back on I had a text message from my associate.

SMS—Transfer Complete. Did you view the contents on the discs?

I delayed my response to his tardy comeback and started the Porsche SUV. I let her engine roar for a few minutes before I shifted gears and joined the clear and red demon eyes I saw from the airbus as I landed. I powered up the dead attorney's phone but it only had one unit of power remaining. I didn't connect it to my charger. My paranoia was getting the best of me and my trust level was 300 feet below sea level. The unknown caller aka Eduardo had some of the same capabilities I had if not more. I wasn't taking any chances of him knowing my whereabouts until I viewed the CDs and spoke to my associate. I wasn't interested in his job opportunities, and the fable tales of his soldiers enjoying their cougar weren't exactly my idea of a good audio book. The satellite towers located the live feed of a dead person's phone and 5 envelopes appeared on the display screen. I didn't listen to any of the messages and powered the phone off.

After two encounters of playing dead man's bumper cars in Tampa, the insulting and impetuous drivers on the 405 freeway felt like Peter Pan's Adventure at Disneyland. I didn't speed or join in the dismal traffic relationships of the SoCal drivers. The sounds of Keiko Matsui numbed me to the blasting horns and blasphemy from car windows. The sounds her fingers made on the ebony and ivory keys were soothing to my ears. I looked at the passenger seat and the duffle bag looked like it was on fire. The contents on the CDs inside were burning through the fabric and staring me right in the face. These CDs must have some information on them serious enough to cause one man to forget all the principles of life, family and happiness in pursuit of the rewards behind them. Another man kidnapped the man's family I killed behind the mysterious CDs and let his adolescent soldiers sexually abuse his wife and who knows the conditions of the little girls. Then he sent an amateur hit squad to kill me and obtain the CDs. Now my trusted associate of ten years was acting peculiar and not communicating with me the same. I felt like a fool mixed up in a game I wasn't interested in or properly invited to without knowing all the rules. I wasn't concerned about the information on the CDs but it had my insides doing triple flips. Would Eduardo give the dead attorney's daughters to me and grant me gradual emancipation with a better security team than he sent for me in exchange of the CDs? How would my associate and the Banderas family react to that transaction and could I handle the possible retaliation? Would I do the girls some good or cause more damage having them live on the run and always looking over their shoulders? Even the finest private schools couldn't keep these goons away. Some of their own children went to the best schools under their father's generous donations. All it takes is one conversation, one wrong name mentioned and I would never see them again and I'd have nothing to bargain with to get them back. It's difficult trying to explain safe houses, escape routes, and a list of emergency contacts to a nine and a six year old already traumatized. I felt the migraine fully announce his arrival. I had at least another forty-five minutes to get to King Louis. I looked in the middle console for some Tylenol. I popped four 250 mg pills in my dry mouth and swallowed them. The left over residue in my mouth was dry and gritty. I didn't have any water but desperately needed this terrible affliction to end as quickly as possible. My temples were pounding like a little person was on each side banging on their first drum set with cymbals.

It was close to 1 AM when I got to my suburban neighborhood. At this hour the homeowners in my neighborhood were either asleep, exploring their fantasies, or committing carnal sins that had no bible or textbook definitions. As I came around the curb I noticed an unmarked black car parked 100 yards from my address. I drove by but didn't look in the direction of the uninvited visitor in my neighborhood. I didn't hit the garage opener to turn the SUV into its haven. I drove past the mortgage-free home and my anticipated rendezvous with King Louis was postponed. The little person's banging started again. In my rearview I saw headlights come on as I continued driving through my neighborhood. I navigated the SUV back down the hill into the city, couldn't have this meeting near my address. More importantly who in the hell was it? Eduardo didn't know anything about me unless of course I had been bartered to the highest bidder by my associate for these damn CDs. When I turned onto Los Feliz Blvd I saw the glow of lights heading down the hill as well. Whoever this was, they weren't good at tailing people. I stayed on Los Feliz Blvd to see if the unmarked car would make the same turn I did. They did and kept a good distance from me. I pulled out my cell and instead of the accepted means of communicating I called my associate. The phone rang but no answer. I didn't leave a voicemail and I didn't send another text message. I kept driving and looking in my rearview mirror at the unmarked car shadowing me. I was almost back to the 5 freeway but didn't want to enter the on ramp. I was really growing impatient with my associate's response time, which perturbed me more. The car behind me changed lanes but kept a good speed and distance from me. I reached under my front seat and pulled out my 9mm. I checked the clip to see how many chances of survivor I had; 15 to be exact. I slowed down to see if my follower would catch up. The driver of the unmarked car slowed as well. He was good. I called my associate again. The phone rang at least seven times before he picked up in a rage.

"What the hell? Do you know what time it is?" he asked angrily.

"Time never matter, now all of sudden you need your beauty rest?" I responded just as angry.

"What is it?"

"There was an unmarked car on my block when I got home that's now following me. Know anything about that?"

I heard him moving around and clearing his throat. He said my name for the first time in 7 years.

"Lance! It's complicated."

"Tell me something I don't know. Who the hell is this following me Ben?"

Now we were both on a first name basis.

"Did you just . . . ?"

"Yes I did so get over it. Who's following me?"

"My guess is Eduardo's people."

"What do you mean your guess? I took a job to find witnesses and shake up a greedy attorney. Now I feel like a worthless pawn in between two drug families and you're standing on the sidelines waiting to see who will come out on top."

"Oh come on, you know better than that."

"Right now, nothing is what it seems anymore. You respond when it's convenient for you. You haven't told me a damn thing about these CDs; you asked if I'd looked at them. Now you're *guessing* who might be following me. Does that seem at all like the relationship you and I've had for 10 years?"

Ben didn't respond immediately. I was angry. I heard him breathing in the phone and felt the devious thoughts running through his mind. I interrupted the pompous bastard I once thought I could trust no matter what happened. His loyalty was now in question.

"Ben, I'll take care of this but we need to meet at ten o'clock in the morning at the normal spot. If I'm not there then you know what to do."

"Lance!"

I hung up after I heard my government name again. I looked in my rearview mirror, the unknown driver still there in my painful view. I floored my SUV to see how interested they were in getting to know me. The follower maintained a good speed and still pursued. My cell phone buzzed. It was Ben but I had no intention of speaking to him until our face to face meeting later on. I saw the sign of a car wash ahead. I slowed down so I could turn into the parking lot without hitting my brakes. Once I turned in the parking lot, I positioned the SUV to face the street and let my window down. The night air was quiet and I could hear the unknown driver approaching. He was driving with two feet; I could hear him accelerate and then stop. He was definitely looking for me and not the 24 hour 7-Eleven. I chambered one of my chances of survival and shifted the SUV to neutral and applied the emergency brake. The black car drove past slowly but stopped just past the car wash. I could see the brake lights glaring brightly, then I saw the clear lights illuminate. The vehicle was backing up. I jumped out of the SUV and ran closer to the street with my gun drawn. I saw the passenger window go down. When I saw the image of a head I began decreasing my chances of survival and hit the unmarked car side mirror and the side panels. I wasn't aiming to kill this time. I needed to know who the hell was following me at 2 o'clock in the morning. I must have hit the driver because the unmarked car stopped in the middle of the street. I approached the car with my gun drawn in front of me with my finger on the trigger. I couldn't see inside the tinted back window. I came around the front of the car and saw the driver's head resting on the horn. The sound was extremely loud in the quiet of the night. I looked around and saw the lights in the neighboring windows come on. I quickly grabbed the man in the driver's seat; he was still breathing but rigor mortis had greeted his passenger. With my gun intimately in his face I skipped the foreplay.

"Who sent you?" I asked.

He coughed and staled to answer. I hit him in the head with the butt of my gun. He yelled out. I grabbed him by his thick neck and asked the question again. I could hear the distant sirens coming our way. He looked directly at me and the words I heard confirmed what I was afraid of.

"Solderota will find you and kill you."

I released his sweaty flesh and took a good look at him. He sat there detached from the moment, loyal to his employers and their cause. The sound of the sirens got closer and my getaway time shortened. I raised my gun and squeezed the trigger; one shot to his loyal brain. I sprinted back to the SUV and backed up in the parking lot and exited a different way. I could see the shadow images of red sirens on Los Feliz Blvd as I drove down the adjacent street. Ben had called three more times. I guess his beauty rest wasn't so important now. I didn't return his call. Instead I turned the dead attorney's phone on. Seven voicemails appeared on the display screen but I didn't retrieve them, I just left the low battery phone on. When I felt I was far enough from the crime scene I turned on Los Feliz Blvd to head home. I looked at the digital clock on the dash: 2:17 AM.

Twenty Eight

It was after 3 AM when I woke up on my own still in Khan's bed. He was sound asleep as I quietly got out of bed and went to the bathroom. There was a set of towels on the sink, but I just wanted to get dressed as soon as possible and get home. I caught a glimpse of myself when my eyes met the mirrored cabinet over the sink. My face showed pain, disappointment, and confusion. The pain from the many dysfunctional relationships I had let myself become victim to. The disappointment in my lack of self-control as I stood in yet another man's bathroom sexually frustrated. Confused because mentally I should have myself together enough to catch the nonsense men throw at you to have sex. Not saying Khan was like that. This was clearly my issue and I needed to get it together. I should have left his apartment hours ago and before we had intercourse. He was definitely charming and appeared to have himself together but tonight I had blocked all of that out for my own physical gain. That had backfired in my face and my mind was on another man. A small part of me felt bad because this wasn't me. Regardless of how others treated me I tried to always do the right thing and this wasn't it. I washed my face and started getting dressed but the mirror cabinet was staring at me. I know I had no business doing what I was about to do but I opened Khan's cabinet. The cabinet was practically empty with nothing more than toothpaste, razors, a bottle of aftershave, dental floss, and two prescriptions. Khan was physically fit so what prescriptions would he be taking? I heard him cough and I quickly shut the cabinet and finished getting dressed. I opened the door to see him awake and sitting on the side of the bed.

"Hey." I said with guilt.

"You leaving?" he asked disappointedly.

"Yes I need to get home."

"You can stay until sunrise. It's really too late for you to get on the road."

"I'll be okay. Do you mind walking me to my car?"

"Sure, no problem."

I could tell he was unhappy. But I had to leave before he tried to kiss me, hug me, or touch me again. I couldn't fake it again and that was the truth. I was no longer attracted to him and we couldn't be just friends. When my car left his parking garage, I wouldn't delete his number; but we certainly wouldn't be meeting again. I couldn't go to that Banana Republic again and run the risk of an awkward moment. I heard him sighing as he got dressed. Was he sighing because I was leaving or because he hadn't crossed the finish line or simply because he felt embarrassed at his lackluster performance? Either way he needed to work that out on his own. I walked to the kitchen and waited by the door because I wasn't about to entertain his sulking or let him think he should get out another improperly fitted condom. He came out of the bedroom and didn't say anything. He just opened the door and waited for me to walk out. We walked to the elevator in silence. He didn't try to hold my hand this time or make small talk. Men and their egos! As the elevator dropped to the parking level, I looked at him. His face was stern and looking up at the digital countdown. I wasn't sure if he'd walk me to my car when the elevator got to the parking garage so I prepared myself. The electronic lift reached the parking garage and the doors opened. It felt a little creepy. He extended his hand for me to exit and stayed behind me. When I got to my car I immediately felt better. I turned around with a smile on my face. His face was still tight and unemotional. I went to hug him but he stopped my motion and went to open my car door. The male ego is truly evil yet men say *our* hormones are the devil. I got in my car and with a straight face he told me to have a good day. He closed my car door and didn't tell me to call or text him when I got home like last time. I started my car and watched the educator walk back to the elevator. He didn't look back and when he got on the elevator he stood on the inside so I couldn't see him. The motion sensor opened the parking garage door and I left the educator and his wrong size condoms. I can't believe he had an attitude with me. I knew my girl Miriam would get a laugh out of this when I told her. If I'm lucky I can get two hours a sleep before I have to wake up and get to work. I will drive in today so I can sleep a few minutes longer. It was 4:05 AM when I got home. I sent Khan a text message letting him know I was home. He didn't respond immediately like he normally does; damn male ego. I jumped in the shower before I got in the bed. Today was going to be another long day.

Twenty Nine

When I turned onto my block the scene was how I expected it to be the first time: quiet with no uninvited visitors. When I walked in the kitchen from the garage, the immediate freshness of the Hawaiian breeze reed diffuser met my nose. I inhaled and exhaled the scent and took in my own space. Catalina kept everything tidy for me. I made my way to my medicine cabinet in the den. The bottle was sitting inside the traditional case it came in with a good dosage amount left before a refill would be needed. I turned on my stereo system and put in a CD from one of New Orleans' very own; Trombone Shorty. The young jazz artist woke up the walls of my den with his booming trombone. I poured a glass of my medicine on two cubes of ice. The smell of the premiere cognac from France was sweet to my nose and even sweeter flowing through my body. My aches and pains instantly subsided and my brain motor supercharged. I looked at the duffle bag on the floor that had the much sought after contents. I had to see for myself what was on the two CDs. CDs that cost a family man his life and all his riches, the CDs that sent two attempts after my life and clearly had my associate pissing his pants as well. I took another sip of my medicine before powering up my Apple electronic brain. Before I met with Ben later on I had to have my next two moves set in place for this unwelcome game I was playing in. I pulled the CDs and the dead attorney's cell phone from the duffle bag. I plugged up the cell phone to give it more bars of energy because I knew the unknown caller aka Eduardo would call. I wanted him to call. I inserted one of the CDs and let the electronic brain download the life or death information. When the information came on my illuminated screen my eyes blinked quickly a few times. I couldn't believe what was before my eyes. I quickly ejected the CD and loaded the other one. More astonishing information appeared on the bright screen. I sat in front of the Apple product motionless from what I had just seen. I opened up the Internet browser search engine and typed in some of the information I saw on the CDs to verify authenticity. What I typed in the search engine all came back first hits. As I clicked on the links, my insides become numb to the recent medicine taken and started doing Chinese acrobatics. The dead attorney didn't lie when he told me what I had is what every drug lord wanted. With Ben's recent aberrant behavior I couldn't help but think he was negotiating his own deal to increase his worth in exchange for the CDs. I never thought Ben would sell his soul especially to the drug game. His circle consisted of rich brokers, investors and a few politicians. He had been the mediator throughout our relationship. I'm sure he got a nice percentage of the transfers I received. It was all beginning to make sense now. Ben wasn't concerned about Banderas or even the witnesses for that matter. He always knew about the CDs at the Clearwater Harbor Marina. I had been played for a fool by a trusted business colleague. How high had my bid gotten between Ben and Eduardo? Everyone had a price in this world; no such thing as loyalty anymore. When people felt you were no longer valuable, you didn't get the courtesy call from human resources terminating your employment. Instead the goon squad came after your life because they didn't want your skills going elsewhere. You weren't valuable to them anymore and they didn't want you joining another team. The sounds of Trombone Shorty blasted through my den as I stared at the electronic brain with the new developments. I wanted Eduardo to call, but as usual his timing wasn't the best.

Before I jumped in the shower I secured the CDs and activated my home security system. It was time I started playing this game by my own rules and doing some negotiating on my own. Why hadn't Eduardo called? I knew a man like him didn't sleep at night or at all for that matter. I checked the dead attorney's phone to make sure it was charging. Now I was desperate to hear Eduardo's annoying voice and learn the condition of two little girls I hadn't ever met. After my shower I turned on the TV to catch up on the local news. I hadn't missed much. There was still talk about the city getting an NFL sports team; two teens had been stabbed in a shopping mall; a guy that used to be on one of CBS' sitcoms was caught on tape making inappropriate slurs. The world news segment spoke on the unresolved issues in the nation's capital; civil unrest in Egypt was still ongoing; and another U.S-run base in Afghanistan had been attacked. Coverage of the last story stopped me midway of putting my pants on. A much younger looking picture of the biracial person I had spent the last few days with was in the background as the reporter gave details of his untimely death. *Details of the high profile attorney Phillip Bach are unclear as Clearwater police have no leads. The young attorney was found dead on his yacht at the local marina harbor. He leaves behind a loving wife and two children.* I stared at the dead attorney's photo. Behind the smiling face I could feel his empty soul bleeding out to me to save his daughters and give them a fair chance at life. The chance he robbed them of. At that moment is when I decided I would not give the CDs to Ben when we met and that our business relationship would never be the same. I wondered what the last ten years had meant to him. Was it nothing more than wire transfers, electronic messages, and infrequent meetings after random homicides? Clearly, that's all it was. Otherwise I wouldn't be in this predicament. I needed to hear the cunning voice of Eduardo.

I grabbed both cell phones before leaving to meet the business associate I could no longer trust. I didn't feel this uneasy the very first time we met. I was more audacious back then and still carrying animosity. Other people's feelings didn't matter to me, the job and the payoff was my only focus. We were meeting at the Griffith Observatory, our mutual respected place where no guns would ever be revealed. This historical location was the site of many school field trips and tourist visits. Years ago we agreed that no matter how heated things got, no one would ever bring the battle or war to this sacred location. Things had obviously changed, so I wasn't sure if the gentlemen's agreement was still in effect. I had two nine millimeters with me and two automatic weapons in the trunk resting with the spare tire. This morning I didn't listen to the radio or any music en route, I drove in silence thinking about the intrepid move I was pondering. I didn't know anything about being a parent. I wasn't exactly the best father or stepfather for the Parent Teacher Association. I hadn't been emotionally connected to anyone in a very long time. When I was they didn't have the baggage, I did. This would be the biggest challenge of my life. Failure had never been an option for me, but this was different. A heroic act of this nature would take lots of meetings with King Louis, lots of patience, and a very good therapist. All three of those spelled insomnia, depression and paranoia. How would I tell two young girls, strangers in fact their father was dead because I killed him and that their mother had mentally checked out after being violated repeatedly by underage cartel soldiers? Was I ready to walk away from the double life I'd lived and enjoyed for a lottery chance on two young strangers? All of these onerous thoughts made me angrier by the minute at Ben, and then my headache paid me another visit.

Thirty

After a quick nap, instead of a restful night of sleep, I woke up and started getting myself together for work. When I turned off the alarm on my phone I checked my messages. Khan still hadn't replied to my text message. He was tripping and upset with the wrong person; but I wasn't about to call and console him. I was just as disappointed trust me, but I dealt with it. Men need to realize that there's more to sex than humping, fast humping at that. Khan forgot about the rest of my body once he got his blood pumping. It was clearly all about him and I had to fend for myself. Granted it was our first time, but damn I at least wanted to see what he had to offer. After I zoned out and took my pleasure elsewhere, the size of his ego booster wasn't really the issue, just his ego. I did have a problem with him going for that Jamaican sprinter's Olympic world record. I'll definitely call Miriam on my first break to give her a good laugh about my letdown from Mr. B.R. I will reply to Lance as well and see if he's serious about meeting up. As I started getting dressed I wondered to myself why hadn't I moved on from this man who hadn't shown any real interest in me. I hadn't spent any meaningful time with him and didn't know anything about him except he had a healthy bank account, claimed to be a business owner and knew one of the branch managers on a first name basis. Yeah, he had pulled up in a nice ride and walked right past the red rope, but there was something not quite right about Mr. Kinko's. I was intrigued by all of these thoughts. Meanwhile the person I thought was going to work out has ego issues, which would eventually lead to other issues. A woman like me needed a real man, a man comfortable in his skin and confident of his abilities. I had no time for the pretenders and thrill seekers who wanted to play out lustful acts from the latest reality show or porn DVD they'd watched. I never understood how some men actually thought porn was real and what they saw could be done just like that. Nothing about porn or reality TV spelled love, romance, affection, or caressing. Most scenes were centered around male pleasure where the woman normally performs oral sex then the man puts her in as many position as he can before he discharges his seeds of life in her face, mouth or on her breasts. So disrespectful. Back in the day, porn was taboo and at least viewed strictly as entertainment. These days both men and women were guilty of using it as a sexual gauge in real relationships. Society had captured and defiled the loving thoughts of men and women when it came to relationships. Dating was no longer about genuinely getting to know a person and then falling in love or not. It had become a game of who had the better online dating profile, who made the next move and was that move good enough to get them what they wanted in the end—sex or money or both. Chivalry was hanging on by life support and the plug could be pulled at any minute. I have to admit Khan had the chivalry department secured. He held my hand and displayed great manners and respect towards me. But I was so annoyed how he handled our first encounter. Instead of talking about it he sulked like a toddler at a new school with no friends. After he was no longer in control, it didn't matter whether I was comfortable or how I felt about anything. He couldn't break that Jamaican sprinter's Olympic record so he mentally checked out and physically his love pole followed suit.

I touched up my eyeliner and put some lip gloss on my lips before I tackled the L.A. traffic. As soon as I was in my car I connected my Bluetooth and called Miriam.

"Hey Jordan." she answered excitedly.

"Girl, are you awake? I need to talk to you."

"Yeah but I'm still in bed; what's up?" her response was eager now.

"Miriam, I've been duped by the charm and muscle." I told her in the saddest tone.

"Girl, stop playing! What happened?"

"He was a good kisser and the foreplay was decent, but then . . ." I paused.

"But then *what*, Jordan? What happened?"

"First he pulled out the Black Label condom."

"Whoa! Not the Black Label."

"Yes the Black Label."

"And then what? Was it expired? What happen next?" she screamed in the phone.

I needed to calm Miriam down before I had a traffic accident. She was too excited for this story.

"What happened is it wasn't the right size."

"Stop playing."

"Nope, then he sprinted for the finish line."

"Oh my God. I've heard of a quick engine inspection. How fast was he girl?" she laughed in the phone.

"He was track and field quick."

"Sorry Jordan."

"Oh girl, it's all good. I adjusted to the skill level of the mechanic and got a little tune-up on my own." I said jokingly.

"That's my girl. So do you think you'll see him again?"

"I really don't know. His ego was really shattered. The aftermath was not pleasant. He didn't really talk to me the rest of the night and barely walked me to my car. When I got home I sent him a text message letting him know I made it. He still hasn't replied."

"Oh girl, don't sweat it, his loss. Did you speak to Mr. Mysterious?"

"He sent me a text message saying he wanted to get together but I don't know if I want *that*."

"Jordan, you can't keep hibernating in your condo. Give him a chance. You don't have to sleep with him."

"What? Am I dreaming? Is this my girl Miriam?"

"Yes it's me, stop playing. I just think you should go out and have a good time."

"And then what you think, I'll sleep with him?"

"No, no, no. Just have a good time and go with the flow."

"We'll see Miriam. Let me get parked and inside to see what the day will bring. I will call you later."

"Kisses and blessings."

"Bye."

Talking to Miriam took my mind off the horrible traffic and Khan's attitude and before I knew it I was in downtown L.A. She could be so calming at times. I thought about sending Khan a text message to say good morning but I couldn't bring myself to do it. I would let this play out however it did. An apology would be due first and foremost from him if there was any chance of a future. Perhaps Miriam was right about enjoying life until the right one came along and not stressing. When I parked my car, I sat there looking in my rearview mirror at myself. My mind was all over the place with good and bad thoughts about my life. The devil's advocate was working overtime on me and I was starting to feel bad about how I handled things last night with Khan. I should've come home after the movie and skipped dinner at his place or left right after dinner. Neither one of us I believe was ready for the physical exertion. I definitely shouldn't have lay in his bed with thoughts of another man pleasuring me. That same man was still loose in my thinking cap and it was driving me crazy. I don't recall ever having a brief encounter with a man and not being able to let thoughts of him go. Lance had cast a spell on me and I doubt if he even knows it. Two loud car horns snapped me out of my trance as two drivers attempted to park in the same parking space. I hate driving in to work. The train would have been much better.

Thirty One

When I arrived at the Observatory parking lot I saw the black Audi A8 that I'd seen only 2 times in the last ten years. As I pulled up to the passenger side I clicked the safety off of my 9mm and chambered a round. I wasn't sure how holy these grounds were anymore. The dark tinted passenger window came down and the face of my usually invisible employer leaned forward. He was smiling like he was happy to see me but I knew he was only happy to get his hands on what he thought I had brought with me. I wondered if he'd still be smiling after our conversation.

"Good morning Lance." he said in a chipper tone.

"Morning." I responded, not as chipper.

"Get in."

"Is anyone in the back seat?"

"Why would there be?"

"Stranger things have happened, especially recently."

He laughed. I didn't get the joke. "Lance, it's just you and me."

Before I got out of my vehicle I clicked the safety of the 9mm then put it in the small of my back and exited.

"Tell me Ben what's going on?" I asked annoyed.

"A lot of anxiety about the CD's."

"What about Banderas?"

"What about him? Without the witnesses it's impossible to get him out at this point."

"Was he ever meant to get out?"

Ben gave me a perplexed look as our eyes remained locked on each other. My look let Ben know I was no longer blind in this game.

"Lance, what are you saying?"

"You know exactly what I'm saying Ben."

"Did you bring the CDs?" he asked matter-of-factly.

"What do you think?"

"I think you need a vacation."

"Permanent or will I return?"

"Lance what's with all of the sarcasm?"

"You know Ben, I was hoping when we met you would be honest with me."

"I *have* been honest."

"Oh really? Then tell me who that was in my neighborhood and how they knew I was back. Besides the rude reservationist and the Stratos flight crew, no one else but you knew I was coming back."

"What about Eduardo's soldiers."

"How would he know anything about me?"

"I have no idea. Didn't you guys talk on the phone quite a bit?"

Ben was downright insulting my intelligence. My face now had a devious smirk.

"This conversation is over, Ben."

"Wait. Lance."

He grabbed my arm. I looked at his hand then at him; he released my arm. His smile vanished. My eyes tightened.

"Do you have the CDs?" he asked again anxiously.

"How much are they worth to you?"

His eyes got big from surprise and he looked out the window. I interrupted his view of the Observatory.

"Ben! How much are they worth to you?"

"Lance, let's not do this. Just give me the CDs please."

"Answer my question."

Silence. I grabbed the door handle and exited the Audi. As my feet hit the pavement I heard the engine start and the transmission change gears. When I closed the door, Ben let the tinted window down.

"Lance, I'll only ask you one more time."

I stood there unimpressed with his lightweight threat waiting for his nervous voice to direct his concluding question. There was silence between the employer and employee but our eyes communicated the new terms of the relationship. There would be no more wire transfers, no more text messages, and no more new assignments. Our eyes sent each other the ancient words of Sun Tzu *"All warfare is based on deception."* When I turned to walk away I heard the scathing words *you'll regret this* then the Audi sped off in the parking lot. I didn't get in my car immediately. I stood there and let his words *you'll regret this* resonate through my ears like I was doing a hearing test and the beeps faded in the background until I could barely hear the beep. Those words stung a little more than I expected them too, but I was ready for the war Ben had drafted me into. I knew he had political muscle but the muscle and resources I had on my side despised his kind to the core. The thought of going to war with him would further complicate the adoption process I had in mind.

I looked at my watch—10:40 AM. I got in my vehicle and headed downtown to see Jordan. It was time to see if she was interested in me. Which one of me was the real question? I wouldn't need her for the adoption application or the initial meeting but I knew she could help me greatly from a female perspective with the girls. I sat in traffic moving like a snail in mud. The dead attorney's phone still had no calls or messages but did have a fully charged battery. Where is Eduardo? Maybe he knew about my meeting with Ben and was waiting to hear back from him. I got off of the freeway and took the streets hoping to reach the bank before Jordan left for lunch. Every traffic light fought against me turning red before I could make it through the intersection. I didn't want to speed and draw attention. I was certain Ben had contacted his affluent public officials by now.

The scene downtown never changes. As I cruised down Temple I saw the peddlers, the barely surviving souvenir shops and some of the best mom and pops cafes in the United States. The cafes had their food and health inspection cards conspicuously displayed, all

Empty Soul for Hire

showing an A rating, never mind how disgusting the place looked out front. I saw the bank ahead on the left as the traffic light on Temple turn yellow. I didn't stop but proceeded through the intersection. A black and white immediately appeared behind me with its bright red, white, and blue lights flashing and the siren loudly blaring. Ben was so predictable. I pulled over and put my vehicle in park. I saw two of LAPD's sleazy enforcers get out and approach. The one on the curb with his hand on his gun holster slowly walked towards my vehicle. The officer in the street tapped on my window with his flashlight. I let the window down.

"Is there a problem officer?"

"License and registration please."

I reached into the glove compartment and got the vehicle registration and the insurance card. I handed the two pieces of paper to the officer. He snatched them and told me to turn off the engine. I heard him tell his partner he was running the ALPR (automatic license plate recognition). I saw his partner nod and keep his hand on his holster. If they searched my vehicle I was definitely going to jail on a felony charge. Ben was really desperate at this point. The officer came back to the driver side of the vehicle and handed me my paperwork back.

"When's the last time you been to traffic school?" he asked sarcastically.

"I don't remember, why?" My arrogance returned.

"You should stop on yellow lights."

"Should I now?"

He stood up and looked at his partner. In the side mirror I saw his partner unsnap his holster. My 9mm was out of reach and if I made any quick moves, L.A's finest would shoot me dead right here in downtown, the cops would be put on administrative leave with pay and plead self-defense at the trial.

"Sir, step out of the vehicle."

Just as I unbuckled my seat belt the cell phone rang. I quickly looked at the screen and it displayed *unknown caller.* It was Eduardo!

"Officer I'm stepping out of the vehicle but I really need to take this call. I've been waiting on the adoption agency to call me back. Do you have kids?" I asked in my best concerned parent voice.

He looked at his partner then nodded at me with a mean look granting his permission that it was okay to take the call. This was the LAPD, the same police department that beat people for taking too long to answer a question wrong or for not pulling over fast enough, but today I was allowed to take a cell phone call. Ben I will definitely see you soon.

"Nice of you to finally call." I answered in a low irritated whisper.

"Oh, were you expecting my call?"

I looked at the phone, then at the police officer. It wasn't Eduardo. It was Benjamin Harper. I looked at the middle console to see the dead attorney's phone still in place.

"Are you enjoying the special treatment from our city's finest?"

"Yes ma'am, I received all of the paperwork."

The officer smiled at me and looked at his partner. He was waiting on a call more than I was. Both of the sleazebags returned to their vehicle and pulled off. I watched them drive by before I spoke back to my one-time employer.

"Is this how you want to do this Benjamin?" I asked.

"You started it."

"No you did when you sent the text about the attorney. It was never about the witnesses. You know it, and now I know it."

He laughed. Again I missed the joke.

"Lance, are you really ready for the big leagues?"

"It's the same league I've been in for the last 10 years."

"Certainly, not. This is the one where the big boys play. Anybody can kill someone."

"Apparently not."

"I've always admired your arrogance."

"You won't be admiring anything much longer."

"Is that a threat, Lance?"

I hung up and started my vehicle en route to the bank. I parked in the garage across the street and rushed into the bank. I didn't speak to the security guard at the front door or acknowledge the greeting from one of the managers. I scanned the teller counter for Jordan but I didn't see her. I looked at my watch. It was a few minutes past 11:30 so I guess she was at lunch. I went and sat in the waiting area for new accounts, loans and safe deposit boxes to wait for her to return. As I sat there my mind starting racing thinking about the many underhanded things Ben could do to me to make my life uncomfortable. He had my account information from all the wire transfers over the years. I stood up and went to the customer service counter to sign in. One of the managers must have seen me because she came over.

"Good morning Mr. Goodman; can I help you?" she asked blissfully.

"Yes I would like to close my checking and savings account."

"No problem Sir. Was our banking service not to your satisfaction?"

"Your services were good; I'm looking to expand my financial portfolio."

"Well we have other banking tools that might be of interest to you."

While she was giving her best banking presentation, I saw Jordan coming from the safe deposit boxes with another bank employee. I stared as she kept walking hoping she'd eventually look up and make eye contact. She didn't.

"Jordan!" I could tell she was surprised

"Ah . . . Lance. What are you doing here?"

"I came to ask you to lunch so we could talk."

The bank manager interrupted to ask Jordan how she knew me. Before Jordan could answer I told the manager we were old classmates from college. She looked at both of us like we were lying through our teeth but didn't press the issue.

"Mr. Goodman, I will have one of the associates type up the necessary paperwork for you to close your accounts."

"Thank you."

Jordan looked astonished from hearing that conversation.

"What time do you go to lunch?" I asked.

"I can go anytime. Lance what's going on?"

"I'm just changing my financial portfolio around that's all. Want to go to lunch?"

"To be honest this is happening too fast for me. I know you sent a text message saying you would like to hook up but I never gave it any more thought."

What could I say? That I had been out of town torturing and killing people? The last time we saw each other was during a bank transaction. These days, people relied on text messages too much as a means of communication. I had become one of those people and expected this attractive young woman to jump at my abrupt invitation. I was wrong.

"Okay I understand. It was nice seeing you again Jordan."

I went back to the sitting area and waited on the paperwork for the blood money accounts to be closed. My anger returned and all I could see was Benjamin Harper screaming in mercy from excruciating pain administered by me. If he thought what I did to Phillip Bach was wicked, wait until those thoughts became a reality for him. I watched Jordan as she walked to the teller counter. She didn't even look back. One of the cell phones was buzzing on my side. I wasn't in the mood for Ben's gimmicks or threats. Without looking at the screen I answered: "Yeah?"

"Amigo Lance."

It was Eduardo and he called me by my name. Damn you Ben!

"Are the girls still alive?" I asked getting straight to the point . . .

"Maybe."

"Still playing games and sending amateurs after me I see. Eduardo, I know what's on the CDs and why you want them so bad.

So I'll ask you the same thing I asked your other Amigo Ben. How much are they worth to you?"

There was silence on the other end of the phone. I was tired of being passed around like a new inmate on the HBO show "Oz." It was time I entered the bidding war and put the valuable information I had in my possession up for bid. Maybe Eduardo would kill the girls to show me how serious he was. Although I was debating taking them, I had no real emotional connection to them. Their death would just add to the countless demons I battle on a daily basis.

"Amigo?"

"We're not friends so please stop calling me Amigo. Answer the questions."

"Yes."

"Yes what?"

"The girls are alive."

"Did you or your soldiers touch the girls?"

He laughed. I was tired of people laughing and not telling me the joke.

"Hello." I screamed into the phone drawing attention from everyone in the bank.

"Relax Lance."

"You've wasted enough of my time. Call me when you're ready to talk business/"

"The girls haven't been harmed but their mother is another story."

"A story I'm not interested in."

"Just giving you a full report."

"Am I supposed to be thankful?"

"You're so arrogant."

"I'm tired of hearing that. There's another question you need to answer."

"I think we should meet."

"I don't think there's anything to meet about."

"You're very difficult."

"What I am is someone who has something you want. The more time you waste, the less interested I'm becoming. There are at least two other parties that would pay a lot to get their hands on what I have."

I lied, but there was no reason to be sincere about with this coldhearted killer. If the girls were still as pure as the woman that gave birth to Christ then I was willing to negotiate. Otherwise my tree would remain branchless and my parenting application would remain unfilled.

"Lance, what do you want?"

"Is it really that simple Eduardo?"

"Tell me."

"For starters an unblocked telephone number."

"Now who's playing games?"

I ignored the sarcasm

"The city and state where the girls are."

"What does that matter?"

"It matters; that's all you need to know."

"Okay."

"Lastly, your friend Ben Harper's demise and 5 million dollars cash."

"And for that you will give me the original CDs with no copies floating out there?"

I didn't know if I had gotten Eduardo's undivided attention or if he was still planning on killing me and the girls, but I enjoyed hearing him ponder my terms so much that I disconnected the call.

A different bank manager came to the sitting area with the documents for me to sign and handed me the cashier's checks from the blood-laced accounts. As I signed my name I took one last look at the teller counter and my eyes met Jordan's. She looked befuddled and aghast. I wasn't sure how to decipher her looks. But I was disappointed knowing we probably wouldn't see each other or communicate ever again. I didn't have a deck of tarot cards, but something told me she would have been perfect for me, and the chance of adoption floating in my mind. My subliminal daydream was broken by a buzzing cell phone. It was an *unknown caller*. I was done taking calls from people I knew blocked their numbers. It was either Ben or Eduardo; Eduardo knew my terms and Ben just wanted to annoy me. The cell phone buzzed again showing the same display. I ignored the call and left the bank and behind.

Thirty Two

Things didn't go as I had hoped with Jordan and now I had a raging migraine. I didn't expect her to fall into my arms but I didn't think she'd be so cold towards me either. Her rejection augmented the frustration of the unfinished business with Eduardo and compounded the pain. I needed some airborne to win the battle my immune system waging. Before going back to the parking garage I walked to the pharmacy on the corner and bought some Excedrin migraine. Coming out, I saw two Dodge Chargers with dark tinted windows parked across the street. I couldn't tell if the engines were running with all the noise around me, or how many people were inside. I slowed my walk to see if they were waiting on me or were they on some other business. One of the devices in my pocked buzzed. Without taking my eyes off of the parked vehicles, I pulled out the phone and looked at the display. The number had a 904 area code in front of it.

"Who is this?" I answered irritated.

"Isn't my number displayed?" Eduardo said sarcastically.

"Yes it is, but that doesn't tell who's calling."

"I have a counter to your previous offer."

"No counter offer." I whispered harshly into the phone.

I hung up on Eduardo, no more games, no more foreplay, and no more pointless conversation was needed. The terms were the terms.

I kept walking to the parking garage, keeping my eye on the two parked cars. As I crossed the street, I could see through the front windshield of the front vehicle. Two men were in the front seat with dark suits and dark shades on. I was almost to the entrance of the parking garage and no one had exited either of the Chargers. When I got to the entrance I didn't break stride. I kept walking to my vehicle and looking back occasionally. If I could make it to my vehicle then my paranoia would subside a little. My vehicle was now in sight and I picked up my pace. Still no one was coming after me but one of the cell phone was buzzing like crazy. I wasn't going to answer either cell phone until I was back in the public view and knew the status of the two vehicles parked on Grand.

I got in my vehicle and started down the ramp to pay and see if my fate was waiting for me on the street outside. I paid the cashier and eased out of the garage cautiously. I looked to the left and the vehicles were gone. As I pulled out of the garage I saw Jordan leaving the bank with another lady. Our eyes met, but no feelings were exchanged; just stares of mutual disappointment. I continued down Grand Ave towards the freeway. I wanted to get home and lie down. I was exhausted. As usual traffic was still a pain in the rear end. I pulled out the dead attorney's phone and dialed the 904 number that I had missed six times. Eduardo answered on the first ring. It was very noisy on his end and I heard a lot of commotion going on.

"What's up Eduardo?" I asked.

"I've been calling you," he said desperately.

"Sorry I was a little busy, but now you have my attention."

"About your proposal?"

"I'm listening."

"The girls are still in Tampa."

"And where are you?"

"My location wasn't part of your proposal."

"Well I want to know."

"I don't see why that's important."

"I didn't think two CDs were so important, but look at the trouble they've caused. So where are you?"

"I'm in Tampa as well."

"Your phone has a Jacksonville area code."

"What's your point?"

"I think you know my point."

"I really don't."

"Okay, well call me back when you figure it out. The CDs just went up another million."

Click.

Ben had played me for a fool and Eduardo still thought I was gullible. At this point I had no more patience. I was ready to get rid of these CDs and see where my life was going after they were no longer in my possession. Would I be on the run for the rest of my life? What about the store? What about Phil's daughters? I really wanted to give them another chance at this thing called life. I would even consider moving and making a fresh start. I had saved enough from the wire transfers but taking on this challenge would require a lot of cash up front. I wanted to stay off the public and government grid for as long as possible or at least until the girls fully understood the consequences we would face as a family. For the first time in my adult life I considered the word family and the thought of it gave me both pain and happiness. I envisioned putting them on the school bus in the mornings and meeting the bus in the afternoon. My evenings would consist of homework, taking one or the other or both to some sport, gymnastic, or ballet practice. All of the things Phil missed chasing the almighty dollar. Now he'll witness them from the depths of hell. Catalina would now have to come in and cook 5 days a week and the cleaning would be a little more than her usual. I was sure she wouldn't mind the extra money. While I was driving home I looked in the rearview and actually saw my face smile. My self-portrait of a smiling family man was short-lived thanks to a cell phone buzzing. It was Eduardo, "Hello." I said.

"That was rude of you to hang up earlier Lance."

"Are you calling to accept my proposal? If not, I need to move on to the next interested party."

"And they've accepted all of your terms?"

"That's none of your business."

"How soon do you want to make the exchange, Lance?"

"The sooner, the better. I'm ready to get on with my life."

"Are you available tonight?"

There it was. The opportunity to make a major difference in two people's lives for the exchange of two CDs. Not just any two CDs; not the latest mixed tape to hit the streets of unreleased music or bootleg copies of a blockbuster movie still in your local theater. What these CDs contained was unbelievable information on a U.S. Senator from Florida and the mayors of Miami, Tampa, Orlando, and Jacksonville. Information detailing the relationship each of these eminent public servants had with the Banderas Cartel and how that Cartel enjoyed immunity in four major cities to transport drug shipments direct from Colombia by air, land, or sea. The points of contact for each city's major airport and Atlantic Ocean port were listed. The CDs had every wire transfer amount to various off-shore accounts. The explosive defamatory information on these CDs was worth more than 6 million dollars but I wasn't interested in a long-term enlistment in this war. Unlike the dead attorney, I wasn't seeking fame. Nor was I planning to go public on Capitol Hill and reveal to our fine government what elected officials in the Sunshine State were doing behind the backs of the trusting people who elected them to positions of power. I was after something bigger than all of that. I wanted the daughters of the man I had killed behind the CDs more than anything and a chance at doing something I'd never been able to do—maintain an emotional commitment to something other than the dubious pleasures of taking another man's life for profit. I had so many demons inside my empty soul that no amount of money could kill them all. A spiritual awakening was the only cure for someone like me. It was time for me to stop running and time to start seeking that awakening. That journey would begin tonight.

After collecting my thoughts, I told the Mexican Cartel leader I was available tonight and what airport to fly into. He agreed to come with the girls and personally meet the arrogant person that's been such a pain in his side. He didn't phrase it quite that way though. I made sure he understood I wanted proof of Ben's death, and if anything looked out of place or I felt any sign of trouble at the airport, then the CDs would magically appear either in the Drug Enforcement Agency's hands or those of another interested party in his same line of work. After I had the girls, the six million, and Ben's death certificate, he had my word that no copies were made. I spent the afternoon memorizing names and the birthdays of Kennedy, the older of the two, and the six year old was Erin. I had one of my local contacts get their birth certificates for me. Ben continued calling, both as an unknown caller and as himself. Taking his calls was pointless so I didn't answer them. He sent text messages as well. Our employer-employee relationship ended at the same place it began.

In six hours my life would be changed forever as I began a new life of being a parent to two emotionally dysfunctional children. I had to battle with the demons inside me either to tell them the truth—that I killed their father or to continue the lie that I was a great friend of their father's from law school. Eventually the question would come up about their parents. I wasn't going through the legal adoption process, so in a way it was a drug deal I made with Eduardo. For years I had killed without conscience but seeing the younger of the two daughters that evening while I was in the Cheval subdivision, something happened to my heart. A great 17th century philosopher said it best—*the heart has its reasons which reason knows nothing of.* This one phrase exhibits the biggest confusion of the human psyche—whether to govern actions by firmness of mind or tenderness of heart. Killing gave me a rush better than any drug, but it had allowed my heart to be unreceptive to love, emotions, and commitment too long.

Looking through the window at the small terminal in Hawthorne I saw the private jet land on the runway. When the single door opened the first person out was Eduardo, I presumed. Next I saw a big and tall fellow step out holding the hand of Erin, the younger daughter. She was dressed nicely and looked clean. At the bottom of the steps she held Eduardo's hand while the big gentleman got back on the jet. Then I saw him come out holding Kennedy's hand and carrying a briefcase in the other hand. My heart started beating fast and I felt sweat under my shirt when I saw the two golf carts approaching the terminal. I didn't have balloons and stuffed animals in my arms. Instead I had a 9mm in the small of my back and a small 22 down by my ankle. I was trying to smile and look excited but this was still business. My emotions hadn't shown up yet for the meet and greet. When they walked through the door I saw the Mexican goon bend down and whisper to Kennedy and Erin while pointing at me. I saw the girls nodding their heads and smiling slightly. I felt the corners of my mouth expand slightly. Five, four, three, two, one . . . two beautiful strangers that I would grow to love were walking towards me. The whole scene was so bizarre and I immediately had thoughts of not going through with it. My demons were getting the best of me.

When Kennedy and Erin walked up to me, both of them were looking at the ground. I knelt down and pleasantly said: "Hi! Welcome to California. Have you ever been to California?" I didn't get a response. I saw Kennedy grabbed her little sister's hand tight. I touched their shoulders and told them we were going to have a great time and to give me a few minutes with the gentleman that had brought them. I walked the short distance to put the face together with the annoying voice I'd heard enough of. He extended his hand and said: "Are you sure this is what you want to do?"

"I'm positive. Are you going to hold true to your word? Or will these girls always be just a phone call away from death?"

"What about you, Lance?"

"I can handle my own."

"Then I'm sure the girls will be fine. Do you have the discs?"

"Do you have proof of death and the money?"

"I have the money but not the other."

The big man gave Eduardo the briefcase. Eduardo handed it to me. I wasn't happy that all of my terms hadn't been met.

"So what are you going to do about Ben?" I asked curiously.

"Ben will be sinking into the Pacific Ocean before midnight." He said confidently.

I gave him the two JVC CD cases and he smiled and told me Gracias Amigo. He waved to Kennedy and Erin like he was dropping them off for a summer visit with a relative. Then he turned around and headed back to the jet. A small part of me was annoyed but I knew I had satisfied the larger of two evils. Eduardo and his cartel were coldhearted killers and he wasn't going to rest; neither would

I have until he had those CDs. Ben on the other hand was a highly compensated middle man now with no henchman to do his criminal deeds. I had been his prize killer for 10 years and his hands had no blood on them. He wouldn't come after me, and eventually his juvenile antics with LAPD would get old.

I walked back over to the girls and asked: "Who wants ice cream?" in a chipper voice.

Erin perked up but Kennedy seemed uninterested. I sat next to Kennedy and asked what did she want to do? A few seconds went by before she looked at me and asked: "Can I go home? I miss my room and my dolls."

"How about we get you some new dolls? And I'll show you your new home?" I asked and reached for her hand. I had gained a small edge with Erin. She hugged her older sister and told her we would get her new dolls after ice cream and stood up in front of her. Kennedy didn't say anything. She just stood up. I grabbed Erin's little hand and I saw her grab Kennedy's as we made our way to the exit. When we got to the car, the older girl tried looking through the tinted glass. She finally spoke to me and asked: "Do you have a car safety seat for my sister?"

I couldn't hold back the smile hearing big sister look out for little sister. I responded kindly with a yes and unlocked the doors. Both girls got in the backseat quietly. As I started the engine I said to myself—Give these girls something you never had: Unconditional Love.

When I pulled out of the municipal airport parking lot, I looked in my rearview and met eyes with Erin. She looked frightened for maybe 10 seconds then I saw her snaggletooth smile. That's when I knew the three of us would be okay.

First and foremost I have to thank God for giving me my mind and the ability to be creative and for continuing to bless me far more than I deserve. Over the years I've shared with so many of you that I wanted to be a writer but my inner fears kept the pen from the paper but the journey has finally begun. So to avoid offending anyone by accidentally not acknowledging you I want to thank _____ for all of your support, your brutal and subtle honesty, for listening to me when I just wanted to vent, for the loving support you gave me when I was really down on my luck, for forgiving me when I embarrassed you or put you in uncomfortable positions, for your encouragement to follow my dreams, for the tasty home cook meals when I didn't deserve them, for the homemade lemonade, for opening your home to me and most of all for allowing me to be *ME*. You didn't try to change me. You didn't argue with me. You gave me your opinion and told me when I was wrong—we cursed, cried, laughed and moved on. I know the road has been rough at times over the years but we continued putting the miles on the Huffy's. Now we're in the big boy toys. You *NEVER* gave up on our relationship, so I say humbly—Thank you! I want to thank my editor. I know I drove you crazy during this process. Thank you for not giving up on me and my story. Lastly, I'm sure I still forgot someone or something one of you have done for me. Charge it to my mind and not my heart because ALL of you have your own *special* place there.

I hope all of you enjoy this journey with me and embrace the opportunity God has given me.

Jan 10, 2013 12:47 A.M.

35.48 N 77.2 W

35 degrees F but feels like 27

Visibility 10 miles

Favorite pro football team sweats, T-shirt from Target, bald head isn't so bald—haven't shaved in a couple of days.

About the Author

James H. Waggoner is a Southern California native, born in Los Angeles. He attended the University of Maryland where he earned a degree in management studies. Although James has had a lifelong passion for creative writing and has written short stories circulated among friends, *Empty Soul for Hire* is his first published work of fiction. A Professor of Contract Management, he currently teaches within the U.S. Department of Defense and lives in Alexandria, Virginia.